"There's one thir Lily said.

Cade held her gaze. "And what's that?"

"We want Gina and the kids to be happy."

"We do," he agreed. "But I'm afraid we have very different views on what they need to be happy."

"Really? I want them to have a home. You offer that to them. But you need support after the storm. Now I have two options for you. I open a fundraising page where I will shamelessly beg perfect strangers to put money into your ranch..."

Everything inside Cade protested. There was no way he was going to let strangers pay his bills.

"Or," Lily continued, "I make a plan for how you can attract more tourists to the ranch and use it as pitch to stay on at the firm where I work. You get marketing tips that would normally cost you thousands, and I get a shot at turning the temp job into a permanent one. Deal?"

Dear Reader,

Have you ever walked through an orchard in full bloom and admired all those tender blossoms? Have you been there in fall when the apples are ripe for harvesting and marveled how such a small white flower can develop into a deep red, juicy apple? Every fruit feels like a small miracle and those orchards, often planted there many generations ago, are symbols of resilience and hope. The trees have to weather storms and survive frosts and if they could talk, they would tell us that after a bad year with little harvest, there will always be a better one to rejoice about.

This story, *Winning Over the Rancher*, begins with a storm and all the devastation and despair it brings to people who have already suffered losses. Staring at the wreckage, they wonder if they still have the strength to rebuild, one more time. I think we have all been there at times in our lives where storms hit and dreams got damaged and we felt like we might never be happy again. With this story, I hope to show that, regardless of the difficulties you may be facing right now, you can overcome and you will find new joy in your life. I hope that the struggles of the characters and their victories will bring hope to your heart and a smile on your face. And that, when you see an orchard, whatever season it may be, you will remember that those trees are whispering to you, and that after bad years, there are always good ones coming that are worth waiting for.

Warmest wishes,

Viv

HEARTWARMING

Winning Over the Rancher

—

Viv Royce

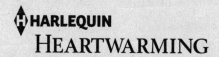

HARLEQUIN
HEARTWARMING

HHARLEQUIN®
HEARTWARMING™

ISBN-13: 978-1-335-47545-9

PLEASE RECYCLE

Recycling programs for this product may not exist in your area.

Winning Over the Rancher

For questions and comments about the quality of this book, please contact us at CustomerService@Harlequin.com.

Harlequin Enterprises ULC
22 Adelaide St. West, 41st Floor
Toronto, Ontario M5H 4E3, Canada
www.Harlequin.com

Printed in U.S.A.

Viv Royce writes uplifting feel-good stories set in tight-knit communities where people fend for each other and love saves the day. If she can fit in lots of delicious food and cute pets, all the better. When she's not plotting the next scene, she can be found crafting, playing board games and trying new ice cream.

CHAPTER ONE

THE STORM HIT so unexpectedly that everyone
on the ranch was caught unawares. There
hadn't been any warning on the weather
forecast, nothing beyond the normal line
about potential thunderstorms, something
to be expected on hot and humid July nights.

But as soon as he heard the wind bang at
his bedroom window, Cade Williams knew
there was nothing normal about this.

He jumped out of bed, grabbed his jeans
and shirt off the captain's chair by the desk
and stuck his bare feet into his boots determined to go outside and see what he could
salvage. He prioritized in a heartbeat. The
barns were pretty much stormproof with
small windows of reinforced glass and
extra bolts on the doors so the animals inside were safe. He didn't want to consider
the possibility that an entire roof would be
peeled off. Nothing he could do about that.

But there were toys left in the yard from his sister Gina's twins, and any object grabbed and flung by such strong wind could do substantial damage. He had to round up anything unattached.

He hurried down the corridor, taking care to muffle his footfalls and not wake his mother sleeping in the master bedroom he had to pass. As permanent residents on this multigenerational ranch, they both slept in the left wing of the ranch house where the family bedrooms were located. The right wing held guest rooms that had been allocated to Gina and the twins. Her old room, still as it had been when she had left home to go to college, with boy band posters on the wall and her prom dress in the closet, hardly fit a pregnant mother of two.

His throat tightened a moment. His little sister a pregnant mother of two. A widow at that. Protectiveness swept over him as a tidal wave just like that day a month ago when Gina had moved back to the ranch after her house had been sold. She had arrived with two crying little girls in her arms, a menagerie of rescue pets and no more possessions than the clothes on her back. She had stood in the yard looking about her as if she was disoriented, not fully realizing where she was and that she was home now. She had lived a totally different life for so long, far away from the ranch and the simple ways she had grown up with. A dramatic accident had forced her to return, empty-handed. But Cade had known for certain things were looking up now, for Gina, the twins and the vulnerable life forming inside of her. Life had dealt them hard blows, ripping all security away from them and leaving them exposed, but their family would be there for them, no matter what it took. This ranch would be their safe haven. The place where they could recover and build a new future.

He had thought that, until now. The wind howling around the house seemed an enemy force determined to throw new trouble into their path.

Cade gritted his teeth as he passed the archway leading into the spacious kitchen. From the shadows a sleek silhouette slunk up to him. Rosie, their Border collie mix, got ahead of him and placed herself at the front door, blocking his path. Her whole stance told him he wasn't getting past her. The rattling of the storm outside made her flatten her ears and he bet she wanted to get away from the door that was being attacked by the forces of nature. But she wouldn't move as long as she was on duty to keep him inside. To protect a member of her family from harm.

"Sorry, girl, but I have to go out. There's work to do."

Usually at the word *work* Rosie got all excited. But now she eyed him like he was out of his mind. Obviously in her estimation, there was nothing to be done outside that door.

She was just like him: determined and stubborn when she wanted something, and he had to reach over her to pull the door open. The moment, however, that he opened it a crack, the wind threw rain and hail inside and whistled past him into the hallway tearing overalls off the coatrack and knocking a crystal vase off a side table. It crashed to the floor in a thousand pieces, scattering the red dahlias like bloodstains on the boards.

Rosie whined and pressed herself against his legs, pushing him away from the door. Her ears came up as she barked low and her worried gaze at him said more than a thousand words. It was dangerous out there and she wasn't letting him walk straight into it.

Suddenly, his mother stood by his side, grabbing his arm. "This isn't a normal thunderstorm," she said, her eyes wide with fear. "This is a derecho."

Cade froze at the word. He had heard about derechos from his father and grandfather. They came out of nothing and could do enormous damage. The last one had hit when he had been two. They had lost most of their harvest and it had been questionable whether the Williams ranch could even survive that season. Along with their trees, their future had been uprooted and it had taken them years to fully recover from the damages.

"No," Cade said, everything inside bucking against the idea a monstrous thing like that would hit the ranch that was his sole responsibility after his father's death ten years ago. "It isn't a derecho. There hasn't been one in Boulder County for thirty years. You're wrong."

His mind raced. The apple trees and flower fields exposed to the unforgiving weather had to provide much needed income. With Gina back at home they had three extra mouths to feed. Not to mention the debts she had come with. Nothing could happen to that all-important harvest.

"I have to go out there," he said hurriedly. His heart hammered under his breastbone. "Maybe there's still something I can do to—"

But his mother clung to his arm, pleading desperately. "Stay inside, Cade, please. What if you get hurt or worse? Who will take care of Gina and the little ones if something happens to you?" Her features, which still carried the softness of youth, suddenly looked haggard in the diffused light of the corridor lamp. "We can't lose you. Not you too."

The pain in her voice kicked him in the guts. They knew what loss was. First Dad, then Gina's husband, Barry. Now it was up to him to keep them safe. It went against everything inside him to do nothing, let the storm tear his precious property apart. But staying in one piece was more important now, for all of them.

He gave in to her and had to use all his weight to bolt the door against the wind that wasn't about to be shut out. It seemed to wail with malicious glee as it grabbed the hanging baskets, his mother's pride and joy, and broke the chains they were secured with like they were cobwebs. His mother shrank under the crashes of them falling, destroying her beloved geraniums. But Cade's mind was on his dahlias and zinnias in the fields. The flowers had to survive the storm, somehow. They were the family's income. If the flowers got destroyed, how would they make it through this season? Pay Gina's debts and provide a stable home for her? This wasn't just about money. It was about family and the promise he had made to his sister and her crying little girls. *How am I going to manage?*

"Cade, come." His mother ushered him back to the kitchen by the arm while Rosie shepherded him from behind. It was as if both of them were afraid he would escape and run outside anyway. To save what he couldn't save?

CADE SAT UP with a jerk. He groaned as pain flashed through his shoulder muscles. He had fallen asleep at the table, head on his arms, and every muscle was sore. He carefully tested his numb arms, moving his fingers to coax feeling back into them. His ears registered something right away.

Silence.

Welcome, wanted, wonderful silence.

A sudden quiet, the absence of all those nerve-racking thudding and creaking noises as the storm pulled at the hundred-year-old farmhouse, shaking the rafters, rattling the panes and howling through the chimney.

It's over.

Relief seeped through his body and he exhaled in a huff. He let his sandpapery eyes adjust to the light from over the stove as he scanned the kitchen.

By the burned-out fireplace stood the well-polished mahogany rocking chair that had been his father's. His mother sat in it; her graying head sagged to one side, chin on her shoulder as she slept. In her arms, cuddled tight against her, sat a little girl, her honey-blond hair pulled back in a braid, her pajamas flaming red against the dark blue nightgown his mother wore. Her bare little feet were tucked under her and his mother's hand rested protectively on her legs. Even in sleep she was guarding her granddaughter like a lioness. That poor, fatherless girl.

Cade swallowed hard. He walked over quietly and recovered the paisley bedspread that had slipped down from the sleeping forms. Ma had brought it from her bedroom to create a cocoon for the little girl.

With a tender smile he covered them both, resting his finger a moment against the five-year-old's cheek. She slept so peacefully now. Despite her fear of the ordeal outside, she had known she was in good hands here.

Rosie, settled between the rocking chair and the fireplace's stone edge, looked up at him. She wanted to get to her feet, but he put his finger to his lips to indicate she had to be quiet, then added the hand gesture for her to lie back down. Her amber eyes followed him as he turned to the other seat by the fire, a big brown leather club chair. Gina had curled up in it like she used to do as a teen, her legs over one of the chair's thick arms. The other twin lay sprawled across her, burying her little face in her mother's warm neck.

Cade fetched a folded blanket from the sofa, unfurled it and tucked them in. He retrieved the stuffed bear that had slipped out of Stacey's grasp and put it beside the little girl. To outsiders the twins were identical especially when they wore the same clothing, but he clearly saw little differences. Stacey had more of the Williams chin. Pa would have loved to hold these little darlings in his arms.

But he had never had the chance to see his grandchildren.

Grief slashed through Cade but he pulled back his shoulders and grabbed the boots he had kicked off. He had work to do.

"That's your problem, Cade," Shelby's voice echoed in his head. "You always have work to do. You live for the ranch and there's no room for anything else in your life. Not for hobbies or for trips with friends. Or for me. We can't see each other that often because of my job in the city and when we can, you have some tree to trim or a cow is about to calve at a friend's ranch and you have to help. You also got elected into some farmers' collective or other, have a meeting to attend or a petition to organize to get the city council to address the dangerous traffic situation on Main Street. I used to like that you did all of these things, were so committed to helping your community, but…these days you're there for everybody but me. I just can't deal with being second best anymore."

She had looked genuinely sad at her conclusion. It had been the reason for their breakup. Not falling in love with someone else, no betrayal, no big blowup. She hadn't shouted her reasons at him in anger or with hot tears. No. It had been a well-thought-out, quiet acknowledgment that the ranch came first in his life and she couldn't accept that.

He hadn't been able to argue with her. In fact, he still didn't know what he could have done to make their situation any different. This was his life. On a ranch the work simply never stopped. He couldn't tell a harvest-ready crop that he'd be back after the weekend. Or a cow about to calve in the evening that she'd better do it in the daytime. And that traffic situation on Main Street had really been dangerous and the city council had just needed a bit of public pressure to finally do something about it. Yes, it took time to organize things, but… he liked to be involved and it kept him so busy he didn't even miss socializing.

"Do you know the last time we attended a birthday party together?" Shelby had asked him. "Eight months ago. I dragged you there. Since then we've been invited out often enough, but you never have time to go."

"If you love that sort of thing, you can go," he had said. "I'd never stand in your way."

"I know." She had sighed. "You don't mind me going alone, because you don't want to go anyway. And you don't miss me when I'm not around. You feel totally fine on your own."

It had been true back then, and it still was. Weeks could go by without him seeing anyone socially and he didn't miss it. After all, he talked to enough people at the farmers' market and the meetings for the ranchers' association where he was recently reelected as regional representative. People emailed and called all day about ranching issues that needed a spot on the agenda. It wasn't like he was a recluse.

Doesn't matter anyway, he told himself. *With Gina and the kids here, there's no room to think about things you want for yourself. It has to be about them now. Solving their problems, making them safe.*

He walked into the hallway, picked his Stetson off the rack and pulled it over his eyes. It always felt good to be able to do something, put his pent-up energy into hard work with a clearly visible end result. It was a quarter to six. If he worked quickly, he might have the yard cleaned up before Ma and Gina woke up.

At the front door he froze. There was beautiful stained glass on either side of the tall oak door and the left panel was broken. It wasn't a huge crack but it couldn't be easily repaired. He'd need an expert for it. *Another bill.*

He opened the door and stepped outside, glancing down to detect what had hit and broken the glass. Something bright yellow lay on the tiles. The handle of a child's shovel. Little Stacey loved to use her own tools to help him with the flowers. For a few carefree moments she could forget her daddy had died and her life was in turmoil. But if the storm had ruined the apple harvest and the flower fields, the safety that Cade longed to provide for those precious little girls would be at risk. *Without money the debt collectors will come after them.*

Even here.

Clenching the shattered shovel's handle in his hand, he crossed the yard. Pink blooms from the hanging baskets were scattered everywhere like wedding confetti. The twins' plastic tractor lay with its wheels in the air and his SUV had a gash on the side like an open wound. His eyes registered it and calculated the damages. But he had two main priorities: the animals and his orchards.

He entered the big wooden barn and walked around quickly. Cows and goats all there. *Check.* Chickens safely settled in their coop in the back. *Check.* Guinea pigs sleeping, only their noses sticking out from under the straw. *Check.*

Mollie and Millie, the rescue donkey pair, stood close together. They had had some

trouble adjusting to their new surround-
ings and seemed to gain confidence from
each other's company. Or was it to avoid
the water dripping from on high? Glancing up, Cade detected several dark spots
among the rafters. There had to be water
leaking into the hay loft. "I'll be back with
the toolbox soon," he promised the donkeys, patting their soft noses. "But first a
look at the trees."

His heart racing, he rounded the largest
barn to get to the entrance into the apple
orchard. How bad would it be? The force
of nature was awesome. Just a few years
ago a strong November frost had killed one
third of all their trees. Cade had been glad
his father was no longer alive to see it. The
family legacy had meant so much to him,
protecting what his ancestors had built
here, gradually expanding the orchards and
adding flowers to their offer. The losses
because of the cold had made Cade even
more aware this was all his responsibility
now. The farm, the family.

What if he couldn't protect it?

The orange early morning light was
kinder than the sharp midday glare would

have been, but still he could see the damage clearly. His boots caught behind torn-off branches and slipped on wet clumps of moss. There were scattered leaves everywhere, loose ones and those still clinging to twigs. Immature apples littered the ground. A young tree had been uprooted, falling over and attaching itself to its neighbor as if desperately trying to stay upright. Its roots reached into the air like tentacles searching for a hold.

Cade sat on his haunches a moment, patting a root as if to reassure the tree. If the roots hadn't been broken, he might try and put it back. "It will be alright," he said in a low voice. "It will be alright." But he knew that even if he did replant the tree, the chances were slim it would survive. Trees weren't made to be broken.

Tears stung his eyes but he forced himself to his feet again and walked on. His heart hammered as he stepped over shattered branches, mini apples skidding away under his soles. If only their most precious tree was still standing... The oldest they had. It didn't bear much fruit anymore. But it was a living memory of the way this ranch had started with his great-grandfather. It was the heart of the farm, of their family traditions. It stood for the past generations of Williamses, their resilience and their hope. If it had been destroyed...

There! Cade saw the tree in the warm morning light. It was still upright.

He exhaled with relief, his fists relaxing by his side.

But this breather lasted but a heartbeat. Something about the tree's silhouette was off. Half of its left side had been torn away. The tree was unbalanced now. Come another storm, it would probably fall over anyway. Because it was no longer able to fight back.

Cade's eyes burned as he stopped beneath it and looked up. This was the very spot where his father had died of a heart attack while working in the orchard. Death had swept him away, quickly. Doc Martins had said that he had probably not realized a thing, had died before his body had even hit the ground. It had been a small consolation. To think his father had at least not suffered.

But now Cade wondered if this was the

place where their family hopes and dreams would die as well. There was so much damage, so much of their future harvest lost. How would they survive this year? How would they make money? It wasn't just him and Ma having to live off the ranch. Gina too, and her twins.

And the unborn baby. Just three months and it would be born. The son Barry had longed to have. The child he'd never carry in his arms.

"Cade…"

He turned round in a jerk to see Gina standing in the wreckage. Her eyes were red rimmed, her cheeks blotched. She pulled the yellow raincoat she had hurriedly donned over her nightwear tighter around her. He had hoped she would stay inside to make breakfast for the girls. But here she was, seeing everything he hadn't wanted her to see. She bit her lip before she spoke again. "It's bad, isn't it?"

Despite her realistic assessment, he saw in her eyes that she craved his denial more than oxygen. His reassurance that it wasn't over for them, in this place. After everything she had lost already—her husband, her home—she had to be terrified.

"No." He said it through gritted teeth. "It just *looks* bad. Wait until I've cleared this mess away. The broken branches, the apples that didn't…" *Make it.*

"Don't fool me, Cade." A tear ran down Gina's cheek and hung on her chin, before dripping to the lapel of her raincoat. "This…" She gestured around them. "Means we have almost no harvest this year. The early and late varieties, all lost. Ma will say we'll just have to be frugal. That we can economize. But how can we ever save money with those debts to pay off? The debts *I* brought along." Her voice quivered.

Cade stood with his feet planted apart, his hands balled into fists. Gina had lost everything she had, her home, furniture, car, savings. All because Barry's sudden death had revealed how much debt he had incurred to offer his family a good life. Several maxed out credit cards, loans… Not to mention the mortgage on their dream house.

The forced sale of the house and possessions had paid off most of the debts, but not all. Gina had to pay those soon or get into legal trouble. He had told her he'd help her deal with the debts this very summer as it made no sense letting them collect interest. But right now he had no idea how to make good on that promise. Their livelihood was about gone.

Gina stood shivering, her hands on her stomach in a protective gesture. "I can't see how we can do this. If Pa was still alive…"

"If Pa was still alive," Cade said with difficulty, "he would tell us that life goes on. And that if we just do what we always do—pick up the pieces and stand side by side. We'll make it."

He heard his father's voice in his head as he spoke the words, saw that weathered face smile at him. *For you, Pa.* "Like we always have."

"Oh, Cade…" Gina hugged his neck. He put his arms around her narrow shoulders and felt how they shook as she sobbed.

Every day she tried to put on a brave face for her children. She played games with them and baked cookies and told bedtime stories. He rarely saw her shed a tear. But now as he held her, and felt how the sighs racked her slender body, he knew she had been hiding her pain inside, fighting the battle by herself. Not to burden them. To be strong for them.

He knew what that was like.

"Hey, sis…" He hugged her tighter, leaned his cheek against hers. "We'll make it. We always have. The twins and the baby need us."

"That's just it." She swallowed hard. "It's harder now for Ma and you because we're here."

"No." He shook his head quickly. Gina should never feel like she made life difficult for them. As if her arrival was the final straw that would break them. Sure, it would be a challenge to get things organized financially, but he was up to it. "We love having you here. Please believe that."

"But the debts…" Her voice broke on the final word. Owing people sizeable amounts of money represented a huge threat to her. Every morning when she woke up she had to feel that darkness hovering at the corners of her existence, waiting to close in.

"Listen to me now." He took her gently by the shoulders and held her away from him, locking gazes. The tears in her eyes broke his heart but he wanted her to see the determination in his face as he renewed his promise to her. Here and now. "We'll find a solution for the remaining debts somehow. You've already come so far. I won't let you fall on the last hurdle, okay?"

Her lips wobbled but she nodded.

"You're safe here." He squeezed her shoulders. "I'll never let you and the girls get uprooted again."

Her phone rang. It had a Sesame Street ringtone the kids adored. Gina pulled it up and checked the screen. "It's Lily." Her blotched features lit in a smile. "When she said we'd stay in touch, I thought that it would be hard because she's so busy with work. And you know how those things go when there are a lot of miles between you. Besides, she did so much after Barry died. She's been amazing while she's also grieving. Her brother gone, the pizzeria sold off..." Gina's features tightened as she seemed to fight new tears.

When Barry and Gina had married, they had taken over the pizzeria owned by Barry's parents. On the list of best restaurants in Saint Paul, Minnesota, it had been a very profitable business and soon Gina, who had been used to rather modest means on the ranch, had been living in grand style: surprise trips, her own brand-new car. She had helped in the restaurant and suggested many small changes to the interior decor. It had been a real communal undertaking for them. And after Gina had become pregnant with the twins and could do less work there, Lily had been asked to step in, temporarily. She had put her college education on hold to do it. Barry's sister had been helping out with the restaurant since her teens. And she and Gina had soon become best of friends.

Cade shook off the annoyance that itched at the back of his brain whenever Barry's family came up. It wasn't that he didn't like them, but they were just...so different. Big-city people who valued outward appearance, prestige. How else could they explain the fact that Barry had spent so much money that he didn't actually have? He had borrowed it to finance the grand lifestyle, not thinking of the consequences. Someday this whole construction of loans and debts had been bound to come crashing down around his ears, burying his family in the rubble. How could he have ignored the danger, put them at risk?

It had been heartbreaking for Gina to learn in the weeks after her husband's death how huge the financial problems truly were, and that Barry had kept it all from her. With the best intentions maybe, not to worry her, but Cade had also wondered if Barry had wanted to avoid being judged for his bad decisions. After all, as someone raised to be frugal and save before you spent money, Cade hadn't really been able to understand why his brother-in-law had borrowed money in the first place.

Lily's call revived the pain and the unanswered questions. With them came a sense of uneasiness, even potential…danger? Because he didn't want Gina sucked back into the lifestyle she had been torn away from. She had to have a stable home now, she and the children.

Gina answered the call. "Lily! I'm so glad to hear your voice. I emailed you last week about meeting sometime but I hadn't heard back so… Oh. How exciting… I'm

fine and so are the girls. We just had a
touch of bad weather last night… Oh, you
know? Has it made the news in Denver?"

He heard a cheerful female voice chirp
on the other end of the line. When Gina
had moved in to the guest room and Cade
had helped her unpack since she was bone
weary from the trip, he had put her photos
on the nightstand: four shots in a single
silver frame. Barry and Gina's big white
wedding, the newborn twins in their crib,
a picture of all four of them on the beach in
Florida and a shot of Gina with her sister-
in-law. It had taken him some time to reg-
ister it was actually Lily. He remembered
her as the wedding planner in the expensive dress who had made sure everything
went down without a glitch. The venue had
been top-notch; the flowers came from a
prizewinning boutique. It had been way too
much to his mind, but Gina had been over
the moon with it all. Still, all Cade recalled
from the day was how uncomfortable he
had felt in his suit and tie and how Lily had
directed everyone where to stand and how
to carry themselves for the wedding photos. One remark she had made had inserted

itself into his brain like a sliver of wood under skin: "It has to look just perfect."

Yes, she probably had a life where everything had to be perfect, flawless, from her appearance to her social media pages. It was something he couldn't relate to, at all.

But in this photo Lily was wearing torn overalls and her dirty hands suggested she wasn't afraid to dig in. At his surprised question Gina had mentioned something about Lily having been a member of the volunteer squad that tended the communal garden. It had been Gina's pet project: a freely accessible garden full of flowers and vegetables for the neighborhood to enjoy. A green haven in the concrete jungle of the city, for people to come and unwind, learn about growing your own food. The rescue pets had also found a loving home there. "I did tell you before about Lily's help with the garden," she had said with an exaggerated eye roll. "You never listen, do you? When it's not about apples or dahlias, you just don't care."

It had been a playful remark, but it still stung. He realized as he stood here that he knew next to nothing about Lily. Had someone ever told him what she had majored in at college? What hobbies she had besides gardening? In his mind she had always remained the superstar wedding planner with demands on everyone for the sake of her social media likes, but perhaps he had misjudged her?

The wedding was seven years ago and people did change. After all, Lily had graciously taken time away from her own life to help out at the pizzeria, the very business that had recently been sold because of her brother's irresponsible spending. Had she also discovered with a shock that Barry had risked everything? And how had she coped with suddenly being cut loose, free to start her life anew? She had only been supposed to help out at the pizzeria for a few months, but it had turned into almost six years. Conveniently sucked into the family business with no room for her own wishes? He had no idea. He simply didn't know Lily at all.

Cade caught himself trying to hear what Lily was telling Gina. But it was impossible to make out much. Gina looked deep in conversation as they kept walking. "Of course you can come and visit," she said. "Nothing changed about that."

What? Cade's mouth fell open. He had just heard Gina mention "meeting sometime" but he had no idea she had actually invited her sister-in-law for a visit to the ranch. Why would Lily want to come *here*? City people might idolize country life, the slower pace of things, and how authentic it all was, but in his experience they often had better things to do in their spare time than drive for hours into a remote area that was beautiful but wild. Although his ranch was situated on the way to the Rockies, there wasn't a lot to do for tourists in this part of Boulder County and they only breezed by.

"Later today?" Gina asked.

Uh-oh. No way. He shook his head and made a cutoff gesture to indicate Gina had to think up an excuse to tell Lily no. It wasn't possible to receive visitors now. *Some other time.*

Gina said, "I'd love to see you. But I have no idea if you can even get here with all the storm damage. There must be trees blocking roads and… Oh, really? You can see all that live online? I had no idea. I never check such things. Fine then. Around ten? Perfect. I can't wait. Bye." She disconnected and lowered the phone. Her red-rimmed eyes glowed with warmth. "Lily is already in the region. She wanted to surprise me by showing up today, but because she read about the storm online, she wanted to check in and make sure it was okay to come today."

It isn't.

"I had no idea you could follow traffic updates online. But Lily knows all those things. She's so digitally savvy. She should be, it's her job now."

Aha. "What does she do then?"

"Marketing. I don't know all the details, but she once told me it's like when people want to launch a new product or give a business a boost, she helps them devise a campaign to convince customers to buy. She presents the perfect picture to get sales."

Perfect picture, huh?

Gina was already rushing on. "Stacey and Ann will be so excited about this visit. They miss Lily so much. We did so many things together back in the city—baking cookies, tending to the communal garden, caring for the rescue pets. Lily also babysat the girls when Barry and I had a date night. They even asked when we were going out again so Auntie Lily could look after them." She smiled, but her eyes also betrayed hurt at the bittersweet memories. "I know today isn't the best time, but Lily's visit will cheer up the girls after they've been so afraid of the storm. I just couldn't tell her no. You do understand, don't you?"

Cade sucked in air to give all the reasons why this was a bad idea. Not just because of the storm damage, but also because he didn't want Lily near the girls. They were just settling in nicely, weren't constantly asking about their old home or their friends anymore. He didn't want Lily coming in for a day or two to rock the boat.

But he didn't speak up. He couldn't say anything about the girls missing their old life to Gina or she'd start crying again. The brief phone call had brought a positive change. She was suddenly smiling and looking forward to something. How could he not be happy when this unexpected visitor had the power to cheer up Gina and the twins? He'd keep a close eye on Lily to ensure she didn't upset the girls with stories about the city and he could always take her aside and explain that they were trying to get the kids grounded again and she shouldn't ruin it for them.

And the mess on the ranch? a small voice in the back of his head questioned.

Well, Lily would be driving out here through an area also affected by the storm so she'd be prepared to see damage.

Still, it hurt his pride a bit that he couldn't show her the ranch at its best now that she had finally decided to visit. After Barry and Gina were married, they had barely come here for holidays. Barry had always had plans to take Gina away somewhere— skiing or yachting—or to go visit his parents who, after handing over the pizzeria, had invested in running a luxury holiday resort in the Florida Keys. He had been happy for Gina that she had such a wonderful life, but he had also secretly wondered if Thanksgiving or Christmas on the ranch had been too simple for Barry and his family. Lily had certainly never shown any interest. Not that she had to but... Now that she was coming, he felt sour that the ranch was in this state of disarray. It felt like he had to show off to impress her and how could he when a derecho had just swept over the land?

His boots were still caked in his ruined apples. There was a mile-long to-do list waiting for him. And most of all, he had poured everything he had into the ranch, everything he was. The damage to it felt like cracks in his own heart. He didn't want anyone to see it this way. Let alone someone who was always hunting for picture-perfect.

CHAPTER TWO

LILY ROBERTS STEERED her car down the road, spying left and right for the sign directing her to Williams Apple Orchard and Ranch. Gina had told her the buildings were kind of tucked away, invisible from the road so she'd have to watch out or she'd miss her turn.

She might have driven past it already.

You've never been there before. You didn't show interest. Isn't it a bit awkward to go there now?

Lily cringed at the critical thoughts in her head. It had never occurred to her before that she should have visited the ranch. The big family occasions had always taken place away from it—Barry and Gina's wedding, celebrations when the twins had been born, birthdays, Christmases. It wasn't like she had been invited there and had not wanted to go. In fact, she had sometimes thought it was rather odd that Gina's family never asked them over. Maybe they didn't have the means to entertain? But even then, a small family gathering didn't have to cost a lot. Or had family relations been strained because the Williamses had never liked Barry? After all, it was remarkable how, soon after his death, they had asked Gina to come live at the ranch again. Of course it had mainly been a practical solution as Gina had lost her home and all, but… Lily wondered if the Williamses had regretted Gina marrying Barry. She couldn't blame them if they did. Barry had really outdone himself this time. With the little white lies and…

Little white lies, huh? Lily's jaw set. Even after her brother had died, leaving his family on the brink of poverty, she still used those nice sugarcoated words for his behavior. Because it had always been like that. Barry was the golden boy. He could do no wrong. Everybody loved him.

Lily bit her lip as she blinked away the tears. She didn't want to think about Barry now or about the complicated relationship she had had with him. She needed to focus on what she was here for. She had realized it might be awkward to show up at the ranch she had never been to before, but still she had to do it. First of all, she wanted to see Gina and the girls, know how they were really doing after all they had been through. A few text messages saying "fine" and "don't worry" didn't reveal much. She had to see things for herself, with her own eyes.

But she also had an ulterior motive. A plan she wanted to share with Gina. She hoped her sister-in-law would agree to it. And that she could enlist her to convince the rest of the family. Gina's mother had looked like a sweet-enough lady during her brief stays at Gina's house. But her brother…

Lily had only seen Cade Williams at Gina's wedding and the twins' birthday parties. He had been the tall, taciturn type who clearly didn't feel at ease with the superficial small talk required at such occasions. He had always seemed in a hurry to get back to his ranch while his mother stayed longer. Whether it was necessary for him to be present at the ranch all the time, or he used it as an excuse to avoid being sociable, she didn't know. They had barely exchanged a few sentences and she was glad for that. She wouldn't have known what to talk about. She had understood from Gina that he had taken over the ranch when their father had unexpectedly died from a heart attack. She had immediately wondered if that meant Cade had been shoehorned into taking the ranch, while he had rather done something else. But perhaps that was her own trauma coming through, of always having to help out at the pizzeria as a teen and then being super glad she could get away from it all. Going to college had felt like a liberation.

Not that she hadn't loved her parents—or pizza for that matter—but she wasn't about to let a business determine her entire life. Studying marketing, she had developed so many skills: photography, presentation, social media, data analysis. It had all come together when she volunteered to promote a big fundraiser for renovation of the college dorms. Her campaign had attracted two big investors and she had never felt prouder of her own achievements. But shortly after, Dad had begged her to help out at the pizzeria once more, only for a few months until the twins were born. She had an associate degree, he had argued, she could get her bachelor's later. And she had allowed herself to be talked into it, then months had become years and… Now she didn't have the funds to go back to college for her bachelor's so she was very lucky to have found a wonderful temporary assignment as a maternity cover that might turn into a permanent position. There was a lot of competition for these marketing jobs so she wanted to grab this opportunity with both hands. Everything she dreamed of—her own career, her own achievements, her own life—was within reach.

If she could get a little help from the Williamses.

Lily bit her lip again. It felt wrong to do this and still she saw no other way. It was her only chance to secure a great job. Other firms might not be willing to hire her without a bachelor's degree and work experience. Besides, turning temp to permanent would mean she could also stay in Denver where she had just settled. Moving away from Saint Paul after Barry's death had been hard enough. She had grown up there, it was connected with a thousand memories. But that was just it. She needed that fresh start away from the painful past, the wrong choices. She needed to rebuild her self-confidence.

And it was so simple when you thought about it. To get the permanent position she had to convince her boss with an amazing marketing project, in the current popular "rural flair" style. All she knew about rural was that her sister-in-law came from a ranch. Said sister-in-law lived at the ranch again.

Go visit, discuss, let your enthusiasm convince her. She can then convince her brother and mother, and bingo, the job is in the bag.

That was the plan on paper. Without all the emotions attached. It seemed doable. Well, of course after the go-ahead, she'd actually need to think of a fantastic way to promote the ranch. But that was what she did for a living. That was the easy part.

The hard part would be convincing the Williamses.

Because if they didn't feel like seeing her, they'd have a point.

Her brother had dragged Gina into debt, and all Lily's attempts to help save Gina's home, to keep her and the twins in their familiar environment, had been fruitless. Big changes had been forced on the girls, on top of losing their daddy.

Maybe Gina felt totally let down? She hadn't shown it, but who knew what she had been thinking? When they saw each other again, would there be the same warmth as earlier, or had things changed for good? Had the avalanche that had killed Barry also buried their friendship?

Lily took a deep breath. She had to stay calm. The accident and the tragedy afterward with the debts had nothing to do with her. She wasn't guilty of anything. She didn't need to confess to Gina what she had known about the financial situation. That wouldn't help her.

No. It would be much better to do something practical for her.

She'd write a wonderful marketing project with the ranch at its heart, get her job and give the Williamses a bag full of tips and tricks to make the ranch more profitable. That was what Gina needed right now: a stable home with a solid financial base.

Everyone would benefit from agreeing to her scheme.

Ah, is that it? Lily hit the brakes and squinted at the simple sign by the side of the road. Made of wood, it had Williams Apple Orchard engraved on it. It looked sturdy and made to last, but it wasn't inviting to the casual passerby. Maybe they didn't depend on sales of produce to make a living? She had imagined ranches in this busy tourist region would offer fresh eggs or harvested fruit to individual customers to earn something extra, on top of bulk sales to supermarkets or other businesses. But it didn't seem like the Williamses wanted anyone to visit the ranch unless they were already familiar with it. That was one of the first things to change. They had to advertise any way they could. "Taste all the flavors of the countryside" or something like that. And they'd have to develop a house style. A brand. Something eye-catching. She'd have to make a few sketches of possibilities and let them decide what they liked best.

Her fingers itched to get started. It would be good to dive in and forget about all the complicated feelings attached.

She focused her attention fully on the possibilities of her plan. "In the shadow of the Rockies," she could call it, even though the actual Rockies were only visible in the distance from here. A rugged outline against the horizon, a breathtaking background for the ranch. The name *Rockies* had a magic pull to it and the drive to reach them wasn't far. The better her plan sounded, the more likely she could interest the Williams family. She wanted them to love her ideas and embrace them, not agree begrudgingly.

But Gina first. Gina and the twins. She smiled thinking of the presents in her luggage. Just a few small gifts to put smiles on the girls' faces. She didn't want Gina to think she was spoiling them.

Ah, who was she kidding? Those adorable girls needed all the spoiling they could get after their father died.

Oh! Lily audibly gasped seeing the flower

fields to the left of the road. She had heard on the news that the storm had struck out of nowhere, and driving over here, she had seen the actual damage: uprooted trees, roofless barns. People had been hard at work to clear roads and make temporary repairs so daily life could continue. They'd need much more time to get everything organized again but these first steps had to help them regain a little control after this devastating natural phenomenon.

This particular field, however, was especially sad. Dahlias and zinnias were flattened to the ground as if a tractor had driven across them. Their bright colors, which normally would have been appealing, now formed splashes of pink, yellow, orange and purple against the rain-soaked earth like a bizarre surrealistic painting. It was a heartbreaking sight.

And in the center of that field, looking about him, stood a man. A typical cowboy in stonewashed jeans and a red shirt, brown boots on his feet, a Stetson shadowing his face. A strong and silent figure like a sentry on the land. All the broken flowers lying about him made her throat contract. What did he have to be feeling, seeing how his entire harvest was ruined?

But was the chance to sell them really gone? Wasn't there an opportunity to do something with the damaged flowers? There had to be. She'd think of one.

On impulse, she parked the car on the side of the road. She got out and waved at him. "Hello! Cade! Hello!"

She glanced down at her shoes. Preparing for this visit, she had dug out the red rubber boots with a daisy pattern she had used in the communal garden and while caring for the rescue animals with Gina and the girls. After Barry's death had blown everything apart and they had all moved away to different places, the boots had been languishing in the closet. In Denver she didn't have a garden to go to, or an animal shed to clean out. She had been job focused, losing her connection to nature. But now she was here and she intended to restore that connection. Her bond with Gina as well and… She had to get back to the way it had been between them before the pain and loss. She had to find a way.

Determined, she began to walk over, mud sucking at her boots.

CADE STARED IN surprise at the slender figure that had appeared from the bright green compact and which had started to plough through the mud to reach him. Her bright red rubber boots with a floral pattern formed a colorful contrast with her white short-sleeved blouse and black slacks. Her shoulder-length blond hair ruffled in the breeze. She seemed familiar.

It took him a few moments to process the information and find the connection. Lily Roberts. Arrived early.

"Hello!" she called again, waving her arm. Then her foot slipped in a wet patch and she yelped, throwing both arms out to stay upright.

He raced over to prevent her from landing in the dirt among the ravaged flowers. He'd probably reach her too late but he couldn't check the impulse to catch her.

She regained her balance in the last instant, gasping as her weight landed full on her left leg. He was now with her and caught her arm. "Easy."

She looked up at him. He hadn't noticed before that she had freckles. In fact, everything about her seemed more defined: the chocolate eyes, the velvety lashes and the curve of her mouth as her lips curled in a rueful smile. "I guess rubber boots aren't the best for traipsing through a wet field anyway. I thought I'd be safe from slips but apparently not."

"Speed also factors into it," he said. "With these conditions it's advisable to go slow."

Her mouth tilted up in a grin. "My father used to say there is no slow mode on me. Even as a toddler I always wanted to run headlong into everything." She looked about her, her eyes filling with concern. "This is terrible. You must be heartbroken."

Uh, what? If a neighbor had passed here, they would have exchanged a few words about the damage, like: could have been worse, have to make the best of it. No one would have said anything about…feelings?

Those he didn't discuss. Not even with the people closest to him.

And she was a virtual stranger. The sister of the man who had swept Gina off her feet, promising her the moon, only to leave her with nothing. He kept telling himself he shouldn't blame Barry as the avalanche had snatched him, but deep inside, Cade did think Barry could have slowed down on the spending and avoided leaving his family in such a precarious position.

But like Lily, Barry had never had a slow mode.

Fighting his annoyance, he said, "As a farmer you care for what you grow so finding the patch like this is a blow. Yesterday it was doing great and now…" He gestured across the wreckage.

"But you can still sell them, right?" She leaned down and picked up a few red dahlias. Anemone-shaped, they were always in demand. "They could… Oh." She stared at the mud splatters on the petals.

He sighed. "Once they're down and it rains, they get dirty pretty quick. I'm afraid there isn't much I can still do with these. I have a reputation to uphold and can't sell customers second-rate products."

She nodded. "I understand. But we can take a few up to the ranch house and put them in a vase I suppose. To enjoy. I mean, it would be such a shame if they didn't fulfill their purpose. Don't you think?"

Without waiting for an answer, she started to pick up more flowers. "Oh, these are pretty." She held out a white ball-shaped one to him. "And what is it called when they have different colors like this?" She pointed at a red dahlia with a circle of beige inner petals.

"Collarette," he replied automatically. "But it's not so much about the different colors. It's because those petals inside the flower—" he came to stand close beside her and ran his finger over the petals in question "—form a separate edge, like a little collar."

"Oh, I see. How interesting." The fascination on her face struck him. She gathered every flower with a tender touch, smiling down on it, and putting it gingerly in the crook of her arm. As if they were so precious.

"Poor things," Lily said. "We won't let you lie here. We can do something with you, I'm sure." She smiled up at him. "My head is buzzing with ideas already."

"Ideas?" he echoed, not understanding.

"Yes. We can turn them into a big arrangement and take pictures for social media and the ranch's website. You do have a website?" She tilted her head slightly, the sunlight catching the sparkly rhinestone in her earlobe.

"Um, no, actually not. We don't really need it…"

"You have to be online these days," she said, wagging her finger at him in playful reproach. "If only to get name recognition. If you'd share a few photos every few days of your work on the ranch, it could interest people for these gorgeous flowers. You could attract buyers, such as flower shops or hotels."

"It has been said before," he admitted, giving her a feigned guilty look. "But you have to understand that…"

"You don't have the time to maintain it." She finished the sentence for him as if she had read his mind. "And you're so right to consider that before you dive in. I always tell people it's not just setting up your website and your socials, but you also have to be active on them to build your platform.

Not everyone can invest the time to do that. But don't you worry for now. I've got my own channels to post to. A few photos and a short video. Yes, that would be perfect. I always let my followers know where I am and what I do. I'm no celebrity of course but I do get good engagement."

"Engagement?" He tried to recall what the term meant exactly. It came from some digital universe that wasn't real. This was: the earth under his feet and the smell of the flowers and…the fact they couldn't be sold anymore.

"Likes and shares." She waved her hand in a dismissive gesture. "I'll explain all of that later. I have to snap a few good shots and post to catch the…" She checked her watch. "Morning break crowd."

He felt like she had suddenly started speaking another language. When she had rushed over to stand by his side and share in his loss, he had felt a brief click of connection. She actually cared for these ravaged flowers.

But now she might as well have come from another planet. He could clearly picture her in the city getting a Frappuccino on her lunch break before returning to an office on the tenth floor of a glass and steel building where her colleagues all sat behind desks typing away at computers. It wasn't like he despised that lifestyle. He had experienced it when in college: that rush to achieve something, have new experiences, climb the career ladder. He had gone along with it, but it had never truly been his way.

His father's death had taken him back to the ranch and that had been a good thing. Now, after ten years, he could honestly say country ways fitted him like a glove. What others considered sacrifice—getting up early, no impromptu trips, little room for hobbies or socializing—was normal to him and something he took in his stride. Being a rancher was simply what he was made to do.

"These peach ones are so pretty," Lily enthused, showing him the cactus-shaped variety he had planted for the first time this year. "They'll be perfect for close-ups."

Her excitement warmed him. He could suddenly see the flowers through her eyes and appreciate their beauty as if he saw them for the very first time.

When they had their arms full, Lily led the way to her car and opened the back. She reached for a large shopping bag and carefully extracted a piece of white plastic. As she unfolded it, Cade saw that it was smudged with dried mud.

"Put them on here." She cast the plastic an almost regretful look. "Last time I used this it was for carrots. They were dirtier than this."

"Oh, you know something about growing vegetables?" he asked. He knew as much from her photo in Gina's room but didn't want to reveal he had studied it closely, taken aback by the change between the glam wedding planner and the garden enthusiast.

Lily laughed. "More about how *not* to grow them. I made all the mistakes one can make: too much water, not enough water, too late detecting snails…" She grimaced.

"Snails can even catch a rancher by surprise," he assured her. "I bet you learned a lot by trial and error."

She gave him a grateful smile. "Thanks

for the vote of confidence. I did manage to get one good carrot that I could eat. I chopped it up and made a hummus dip to go with it and I enjoyed my reward to the full."

He held his head to the side. "You were happy with that one carrot?"

"To you it might seem a little silly." She shrugged, as if embarrassed. "But I put a lot of time and energy into my bit of the communal garden and I did want to see a result. *Any* result. I'm like that with everything I try. If I do climbing, I want to make it to the top of the wall." She grinned. "Even if I lose all the skin on my hands."

Involuntarily, he glanced down to her hands that looked pretty pristine.

Lily flushed. "I haven't had the chance to do any climbing lately. Or other hobbies. Haven't seen earth up close after leaving the communal garden project behind in Saint Paul when I moved to Denver for a new job. Since then it's been all about work really."

He could so relate to that.

She continued, "I'm hired for a few months only as a maternity cover. But I intend to stay there. I just need to convince them that I'm that good." She smiled, looking at the flowers they had piled into the car. "There, they look so pretty. Now I have to think of a stunning way to photograph them. Something that draws immediate attention." She scrunched up her face, drawing her brows together. Even her nose wrinkled.

Wait a minute. She had breezed onto his ranch, picked up his flowers and was going to photograph them for her social channels to get likes on her posts. This wasn't how he had pictured her visit to pan out. He had imagined himself staying out of her way and letting his mother and Gina show her around. If she even wanted to see the ranch. He had seriously doubted that she'd have any interest in flowers or apples. Now she had asked questions about the different varieties and stood ready to use the dahlias in a photo shoot. Admittedly, it was great she appreciated what he grew here, but did he really want to be part of this race for engagement, the whole fast-lane life her brother had been so good at?

Considering how that had ended for Gina, it made his mouth go sour.

He cleared his throat. "You drive to the ranch house. I'll walk." He needed a few minutes away from her to think of a way to forbid her to do this. He had been caught off guard, but he'd do something about that. *Right away*.

She snapped those big brown eyes up at him. "Do you think you don't fit into my tiny car? Some people call it the grasshopper because of the color."

"I wouldn't dare insult it," he assured her. Her sense of humor shone through, and he had to admit that after Gina's mention of marketing as Lily's career he had sooner expected her to arrive in a businesslike dark blue sedan. Or maybe something more expensive like the cars Barry had loved, to fit in with a certain lifestyle? But then he knew next to nothing about marketing people. Not even what they did *exactly*.

"Come on," she said and walked to the driver's-side door. He opened the other door and folded his tall frame into the passenger seat. In the narrow space he struggled to buckle up. She snapped her own seat belt in place. She wore a bracelet with rhinestones matching the ones in her earrings. Everything about her seemed to sparkle, especially her eyes.

He looked for something casual to say but didn't seem to find a convenient topic. Small talk had never been his thing. It wouldn't be long before she figured out that he wasn't exactly a star at engaging conversation. A few awkward silences and they'd reach the ranch house. Just a few minutes.

Lily turned the ignition on and the radio started playing.

A rock station? "Is that what you like to listen to?" he asked before he really thought about it. "Not that there is anything wrong with it," he rushed to add. "I mean, tastes do differ. And just because you look so…" *Stop putting your foot in it, Cade.*

"I won't ask what you mean." Her voice quivered with suppressed laughter. "But my musical taste is different every day. Sometimes I'm in the mood for big band and then for classical. You know?"

She snapped off the radio and said, "Maybe I shouldn't have come today of all days. You must have a ton to do. I did ask Gina whether it was okay to go through with the visit after the storm, but… People sometimes think I'm a little too spontaneous." She pursed her lips. "I guess it's because I get excited about an opportunity. I hope you don't think it was too forward of me to want to come over? I mean, it's not like I've often been here before."

And there it was, the awkward silence. And now he almost wished it was because of his lack of social graces. But this was much more. Lily had never been here before, because her brother had always made sure family gatherings happened with his family, in their world, with rich and successful friends. The invitations Ma had sent them, for Thanksgiving or Christmas, had always been declined by a remorseful Gina who explained Barry had already arranged for something, booked a trip, whatever. Almost like he had been embarrassed to come here for the holidays and see the humble origins of his wife?

He couldn't ask Barry anymore why it had been that way. And he certainly couldn't ask Lily. First of all, she didn't need to defend her brother and second... he'd hate to discover she was just the same.

Had she come to see if Gina and the

twins even had a normal life here? Was she worried they were lacking in something? Big-city thrills, diversions, friends?

"Gina said it was okay to come," Lily said, giving him a worried glance.

He realized she was waiting for a reply to her question whether she had been out of line inviting herself here. Maybe, but somehow he couldn't bring himself to say it.

"Oh, it's okay," he said lamely. He had to recall Gina's happy expression when she had taken Lily's call. She did want to see her sister-in-law and that was what mattered. He'd have to deal with his own issues, keeping his unease to himself.

He added, "I uh…just don't see what we can do with the flowers. Actually, I uh…had meant to keep the extent of the damage away from Gina and my mom. It's never nice seeing the things you care for go to waste."

"But they aren't going to waste. I'm going to make them useful somehow. Just wait and see." She nodded at him. Her eyes searched his expression as if she wanted to know a ton about him but didn't know quite where to start.

"Keep your eyes on the road," he urged her as she almost skidded into the side bank.

"Sorry. I'm not used to dirt roads. Don't you think it's lonely living like this?"

Lonely, yes, that was always the first thing city people figured. "Not really." He wanted to explain to her what it was like to be out in the orchards at night and look up and see the universe stretch above him, with tiny specks of stars and the bright light of Venus, and feel so small and yet so much a part of everything that was alive.

But he didn't really know how to say that, explain it so she'd understand. Judging by all the places Barry had taken Gina and the kids, Lily had probably also seen her fair share of the world, admired dazzling sights that made the night sky over his orchard fade by comparison. "I'm used to it," he just said with a shrug. "I grew up here."

"And you never wanted to do anything else?" She glanced at him, again probing into his very soul with that superinterested look. Why did she want to know things about him?

During their previous brief encounters she had never shown any interest in his life. Was it because she was on his territory now? Felt obliged to ask some polite questions, to make conversation? Some people couldn't stand silence and felt they had to fill it with small talk.

The car skidded again, and she looked back ahead, saying, "Eyes on the road, yes, sir."

He suppressed an involuntary grin. She was a whirlwind he did welcome. A breath of fresh air they could all use on this sad day.

But her question if he had never wanted anything else lingered. He had never regretted taking over the ranch. He was cut out for this work and he was one with the land. But the constant demands on his time meant other areas of his life went neglected. Especially the one labeled personal relationships. Other men his age had wives and kids. Having Gina's little ones around reminded him all the more how he'd always thought he'd be a father before turning twenty-five. Now at thirty-two there wasn't an engagement ring in sight, let alone a wedding band and a baby cradle.

"Um, I'm sorry if I touched a sore spot,"

Lily said beside him. Her voice was gentle, inviting him to share if he wanted to.

He jerked back to the present, realizing he was stalling with his answer, even though it was a very simple one. "I love the family business," he said. "I'm the fourth generation tending it."

THAT WASN'T REALLY an answer, Lily thought, but she didn't say anything. Gina had never told her much about her older brother and she supposed that there was a reason for that. Or it had merely not occurred to Gina that Lily was interested in him.

Which I am not, she told herself sternly. Cade Williams's looks might fit her profile of a handsome man to perfection but he hadn't exactly been approachable, back then at the wedding or right now. She did understand he'd had a rough night with the storm and probably had a head full of to-do lists for the coming days, but still there seemed to be more behind his guarded behavior around her.

As if he was wary why she was really here.

Or was she just projecting suspicion

on him because she knew she had something more in mind than checking up on her sister-in-law? The ranch's location in the shadow of the Rockies could be perfect for her marketing project, to turn her temp assignment into a steady job. She had to explore that opportunity. If she could stay here for a few days, she could also have a heart-to-heart with Gina, figure out how she and the girls were really doing. And she wouldn't be fobbed off with a casual reassurance everything was fine. Even if that was easier, because talking about Barry was so hard. The idea of having to do it made her stomach squeeze. She couldn't allow herself to cry and show weakness to Gina. She had to be strong for her, know all the answers.

"Here we are." Cade gestured ahead into a yard with a large white house to the right and wooden sheds and barns across from it and to the left of it, in an L shape. She didn't see any animals but supposed they were still inside. Despite the visible traces of the storm's violence, the house looked gorgeous in the summer sunshine: all whitewashed wood, with a central oak front door and man-size stained glass panels on each side of it depicting apples.

Cade had gotten out already and rounded the car to open the door for her. A real old-school gentleman. It gave her a fuzzy feeling inside to be treated with such attention. As she stood beside him, their gazes locked for a moment, and her stomach reacted like she was on a swing sweeping her high through the air. This girl who always had solid ground under her feet was suddenly flying.

CHAPTER THREE

A LOUD *HEE-HAW!* rent the air and Lily turned her head. "That's Millie. Or Mollie. I can never tell their voices apart. But it seems like…"

They know I am here. She bit back the words. Of course the donkeys couldn't know that, not from behind a wooden wall. But she so wanted to pet these sweet rescues she had once saved with Gina. When Gina moved back home, the animals had gone with her and the kids, and Lily had only seen photos of them in their new stable. It wasn't the same as feeling their soft fur under her fingertips. She really wanted to hug them again.

"I bet they'll be happy to see you," Cade said, adding after a moment, "As long as you bring a carrot."

She made a slapping gesture at him. "Don't make them sound so self-serving. Those animals are very sensitive to the world around them. Did you know donkeys can read people's posture and deduce their mood from their body language?"

"Really? How did you find out about that?"

"The hard way when I did a donkey walk as a team-building exercise. You hike for a stretch with a donkey as your companion. They either trust you and follow along or they don't believe in you at all and refuse to go anywhere. It all depends on self-confidence. The donkeys' behavior revealed something about our roles in the team. After the walk we got feedback and advice about what we could change and apply to a work situation. It was fun."

She wasn't going to tell him that at the time her self-confidence had been so low the donkey hadn't wanted to lift a hoof to follow her. She had felt like a total impostor, but fortunately, her colleagues hadn't done much better. They had all been able to laugh at their struggles and take the advice for improvement to heart.

Cade tilted his head. "I wonder what they deduce from my body language. They always give me a hard time when I want to lead them."

"That's because they don't like coercion. If you start pulling when they don't want to go, they dig in and you can't move them. But if you let them figure it out for themselves, give them a little space to explore…"

The front door opened and Gina appeared, in a blue dress with her strawberry blonde hair loose over her shoulders. She looked radiant. If Lily hadn't known she had recently lost her husband and her home, she would have believed this was a perfectly happy pregnant woman enjoying a day out in the country.

It never ceased to surprise her how well Gina masked her pain. Why would she anyway? They were such good friends she needn't play pretend, right?

Or was Gina afraid to tell her the truth about how mad she was about Barry's choices, the debts, the way in which her entire life had been ripped apart? Maybe Gina didn't say a word about it to spare her. But what if she ever found out Lily had known about the debts? Well, at least about some of them…

Lily's heart sank at the idea that Gina would find out and hate her for it. She had always enjoyed their friendship. They had grown so close caring for the twins and sharing the load of the responsibility for the restaurant. It had almost felt like Gina had been her sister. The sister she had never had. To think she might tell her to her face she hated her...

That would really break her heart. She had tried so hard to help.

But maybe that had been her crucial mistake. That she had always helped out and never allowed Barry to face the consequences of his acts. That might have made him worse. Maybe he had pushed further, had taken more risks, because he had never fallen on his face. If he had hit a brick wall sooner, maybe it would never have come to the financial disaster that had caused the sale of the restaurant, the house, everything... Maybe in always cleaning up for him, she had let him down?

It felt like that. As if she had failed Barry, their parents, Gina and the kids. She tried not to think of it most of the time, because if she allowed herself to face it, an abyss of guilt and regret opened up that would swallow her alive.

"Hello!" She sank to her knees and spread her arms wide for the two little girls running toward her. They wore identical yellow dresses with yellow bows in their shoulder-length blond hair. One of them half fell, but the other raced ahead to hug Lily. "Hello, Aunt Lily. It was so scary last night. The thunder came to catch us."

Lily held her by the shoulders and looked her in the eye. Judging by the chin, it was Stacey. She hadn't noticed before it was Cade's chin. She smiled as she said, "But Uncle Cade was there to keep you safe, right? I bet the thunder is afraid of him."

She glanced up to where Cade stood. He playfully balled a fist at Stacey to show off. His blue eyes twinkled.

But Stacey didn't smile. With a serious expression she said, "It went away quickly. But the rain was so loud we couldn't sleep. Mama sat with me by the fire. And Ann was with Grandma."

Ann had caught up and pulled at Lily's arm to get her attention. "Did you bring us presents?" she demanded.

Cade burst out laughing. "That's for sure the first thing we need to know. If you didn't bring presents, you can't come inside."

"Cade!" Gina warned, approaching quickly. She added to her daughter, "You don't ask guests questions like that."

"Aren't you glad to see me without presents?" Lily asked softly, putting her finger to the little girl's button nose. Kids always wanted presents; she had brought them for that exact reason. Still she ached to know she was welcome here regardless of what she'd brought.

Ann tilted her head, considering the question seriously. "Sure," she said with a generous smile, "I want to show the ranch to you. Where we put the guinea pigs. We have a new one. It's white and orange. It doesn't have a name yet. Maybe you can think of one. You always think of good names." She glanced at her mother and added, "But we do need presents. Mama was crying this morning."

Lily looked up at her friend. Gina's eyes were dark as if it only hit her now that her children might have noticed her sad mood. "I wasn't really crying," she said quickly, in a forced cheerful tone. "I was just tired from sitting up at night and rubbed my eyes too much."

Lily caught Cade's worried look at his sister. The laughter that had relaxed his features moments ago when he was teasing about the presents was wiped away and pain pulled his jaw tight. She wished she could put her hand on his arm and tell him she'd help him cheer up Gina and the twins. That two heads were better than one and they'd think up ways to make this an amazing summer.

Summer? She was only staying a few days. To gather material for her project.

If they even agreed to a project.

"Mama *was* crying," Ann repeated with determination and leaned into Lily, a lost expression on her young face.

Lily bit her lip. She ached for an easy answer to make the girl laugh again. But there wasn't any. Her mother was crying because their father had died. It had to feel like nothing in the world made sense anymore. And over time it would get a little better, the sharp edges might wear off, but grief could always hit out of the blue like their feet getting knocked out from under them. She never stopped thinking that if Barry hadn't died, everything would have been so different. For her, for Mom and Dad, for Gina and the children. That unborn baby that would never get to know his father.

But no, she didn't want to think about that. *Not now.*

She put her arm around the girl's narrow shoulders. "Then I have everything here to make you smile again. Presents *and* candy."

"Hurrah!" Stacey jumped up and down. The bow on her head sagged to one side. Gina loved to dress up the little girls but their wild antics ensured that the effect was often short-lived. Having been a bit of a tomboy herself, Lily could sympathize. Still, for Gina's sake she straightened the bow. The girl shifted impatiently under her touch. "Can we have our presents now?" she pressed.

"We should first bring our guest inside and offer her some banana bread," Cade corrected quietly but firmly. "Grandma baked it fresh for Lily." He caught her eye. "It's the best in the county."

"Oh, she shouldn't have really," Lily said.

"I'm sure you had other things on your mind." She hoped her visit hadn't caused any more bustle.

"Come on. You've got to see Rosie. She's so cute." Stacey took Lily's one hand, Ann the other. It was so good to feel those small fingers in her palms again. She had missed them so much.

They pulled hard to drag her up the porch steps and inside, into the mouthwatering scent of something sweet straight from the oven. A woman in her fifties, dressed in a lavender blouse and black jeans, her graying hair swept back into a ponytail, came to meet them carrying a large plate with slices of banana bread. Her features resembled Gina's to a tee.

"I was about to take it outside," Mrs. Williams said with a smile. "Welcome to the ranch, Lily. It's been ages since we last saw each other. Come into the kitchen. That's the place where we pretty much live through the day."

She said it almost apologetically, but Lily understood why they'd choose to when she entered the kitchen. It was so spacious and gorgeously lit by the morning sun streaming in through the windows. The huge sinks, the classic stove and the wooden floorboards could come straight from a country life magazine, but the many kids' drawings tacked to the fridge and a sweater left over the back of a chair showed the space was truly lived in. It welcomed her into a hug.

Mrs. Williams asked, "I hope the drive wasn't too hard despite the storm damage?"

"The road was pretty good. They must have been up early to clear it. I also saw people clearing away wreckage in towns I passed and in the fields. Everybody seems determined to resume normal life as soon as possible. Are these storms common here?"

"Not of this intensity," Mrs. Williams said. "Have some banana bread."

Lily sensed the older woman didn't want to talk about the storm right now and accepted the sweet treat. "It's delicious," she said around her first bite. Her gaze fell to an array of colorful postcards stuck to the fridge. They came from places all over the world. Gina saw her looking and said, "April sends those."

April was Cade and Gina's younger sister. Lily had only met her briefly at the wedding.

Gina continued, "When she became a cruise attendant, she promised us a card from every new harbor where her ship docked and so far she's been true to her word."

Mrs. Williams said, "We should message her that we're okay in case she hears about the storm and is worried for us."

"Already done." Gina gestured for Lily to sit down at the large square table. All eight ladder-back chairs around it had checkered pillows in blue and white.

"How long will you be staying?" Mrs. Williams asked. "Gina told me you had been talking about a visit for a while?"

Gina said, "Yes, I should have told you, but it completely slipped my mind."

"It was a rather impulsive decision on my part to come today," Lily said. She was glad she could focus on the banana bread and didn't have to look Mrs. Williams in the eye. She suspected the woman could see right through her and know she was here for another reason than merely visiting Gina and the girls. "I also wanted to see the area. In my work I have to come up with ideas all the time so inspiration is essential. And such a wonderful rural area provides it by the buckets."

"I can't imagine big-city people being interested in the trends of the countryside." Cade stood in the archway leading into the kitchen. "Do we even have trends or are we all stuck in the last century?"

His hostile tone took her by surprise. But maybe someone had once made a barbed comment and he thought she felt the same way? "On the contrary," she rushed to explain. "Rural influences are very on trend at the moment. People want to experience the peace and quiet of the countryside, have a bit of slow living. They idealize such environments as this."

"Probably because they don't know them at all." Cade sounded cynical. "They picture us ranchers lying in a hammock all day long watching the blue skies."

Gina said quickly, "I bet that Denver firm who hired you as a maternity cover will keep you on for a permanent position, in a heartbeat. You are that good. And your enthusiasm is infectious."

"I guess I need to convince them with more than a good idea. I need to develop a solid pitch project. Some big thing. I guess that… I also came this way looking for it." She thought it better to suggest she was searching in the area and then zoom in on the ranch as a possibility.

Cade laughed softly. "Really? You think some farmer around here has the money to hire a city marketing specialist?" He walked to the sink to wash his hands. "I guess some people would have liked to expand into the tourist industry, but after this storm nobody will have the funds to do so."

She couldn't make out if he was relieved by that, or disappointed. If he had considered getting outside advice to boost his ranch, she might find an open door here to offer her help.

"Not every change needs to be super expensive," she explained. "You can work with what you've already got." She gestured with both hands. "Take a ranch like this one. You could offer people a chance to pick their own bouquet of flowers, or their own fruit. Once they're here you can entice them to buy produce in your own farm shop."

"Farm shop?" Cade echoed. He half turned to her, with dripping hands, holding her gaze. "Do you think I have the time to stand behind a counter selling stuff?"

"I said before we could sell some things here," his mother said. "It need not go through the farmers' market alone."

"Yes, but we'd need adjustments for that and everything costs money."

"We could run a small pilot. Just to see if it works." Lily looked at Gina. "We did discuss before how you could do something at the ranch for families."

"I remember." Gina nodded. "You said that the children of those families who'd come to pick a bouquet—and you assumed there'd be a lot of families, you know as the Rockies are a real family destination—would love to pet donkeys and goats. We could have a petting zoo again, like we used to in Saint Paul." Her voice carried a sharp longing that tugged at Lily's heartstrings. She knew what it was like to ache for something you lost, for times when you had been happy.

"And we could offer tours of the orchards," Mrs. Williams added. "To teach children how apples develop from the flower in spring to the fruit in fall." She looked at Cade. "Your father had an idea to do something with education, but when he died…"

Cade grabbed a towel and rubbed his hands dry. Lily couldn't read his emotions from his stance. Did his shoulder muscles merely move because he was toweling so hard, or was he getting worked up about all these ideas?

Maybe it was the wrong moment, after last night's devastating storm? She could well imagine it was hard to have someone march in with upbeat ideas while your heart was bleeding over what you had built and lost. Again she felt the urge to touch him and tell him it would be okay. But a strong man like him probably didn't even need that kind of support. He'd be used to fending for himself.

"I was just painting a picture," she said quickly, "of what one could do. To give you an idea of what I might pitch to the firm in Denver." She suddenly felt a little lost sitting at the table, picking at her banana bread. They knew about life here; she didn't. Was she overreaching, thinking she could help out? All because she had helped Cade pick up his broken flowers.

"Oh…" Reminded of the dahlias in the back of her car, Lily flew to her feet. "I have a photo session to do. Who wants to help me?"

The girls raised their hands in unison. "Me, me, me!"

"We're going to put the flowers in a basket and then you can carry the basket and I'm going to snap you from behind." She looked at Gina. "If it's alright with you to share a photo of the children. Their faces won't be visible."

Gina nodded. "Okay with me. We did it for the communal garden so why not?"

"Great. Come on, girls. You better put on some rubber boots. I assume you've got some?"

"A whole assortment of them," Cade said.

"You got your daisy boots from the garden," Ann said to Lily before rushing off to find her own.

CADE SAW THE flash of pain across Lily's features when Ann mentioned the garden. She had also looked sad when she said she hadn't been able to do any gardening once she had moved to Denver for that job. Was she working too hard? Trying to prove herself?

Why had he been so prickly at her suggestion she could do something for them? Just because he thought it would create more work while he was already stretched to the limit with repairing all the storm damage? She was obviously enthusiastic and a hard worker. Besides, Ma was right. Pa had wanted to do something with education before he died. To try and fulfill that wish of his would be a nice thing to do this summer. Something positive for them as a family after their recent loss.

Rosie pressed herself against Lily's legs, looking up at her. The dog was usually attuned to feelings. The moment she sensed someone was unhappy she came over to offer her support.

"Hey, girl." Lily rubbed the dog's head. "She's too cute. As a kid I always wanted a dog. But we couldn't have one because of the restaurant. Mom and Dad worked long hours and they didn't think us kids could take care of a pet on our own. On top of homework and household chores." She grimaced. "I kept asking Santa for a puppy. But whatever he brought it was never that dog."

"Sorry to hear that. To the girls Rosie is the perfect cuddly buddy, but she's also a working dog." Cade made a hand gesture to Rosie to separate her from Lily. The dog hesitated a heartbeat as if the order clashed with her own inner conviction that this human needed more support. But when Cade repeated the gesture, she detached herself and sat up watching him intently to see what he wanted of her next.

Lily whistled. "I'm impressed. You don't even have to say a word. Can she do compound commands too?"

"Now *I'm* impressed. You know something about dog training with compound commands?"

"I saw it on TV once." She shrugged. "It's not like I have personal experience with it."

"Well, it's never too late to learn. But I'm telling you one thing. Rosie is a very smart girl. If she feels like your command is pointless, she will think of a better one herself."

Lily laughed, her head back. It was such a happy carefree sound. He was relieved her sad mood had evaporated.

Cade pretended to be hurt. "I mean it. She makes you feel you're not in her league at all."

"Example?" Lily held his gaze.

Cade didn't have to think about that one. "We were at a training session. All dogs had to jump in the water of an artificial pond, swim to a platform on the other side of the water, pick up a dummy and swim back. Rosie dived in, swam ahead of the others to the platform, picked up the dummy, crawled out of the water and ran around the pond to reach me. She realized that running around the pond was faster than swimming back."

"Clever girl." Lily clapped her hands together.

"We got disqualified for not playing by the rules." Cade grimaced. "I tried to explain the dog simply chose the better option to complete the task as fast as possible, but the trainer didn't want to hear it."

"How narrow-minded." Lily leaned down to scratch Rosie behind the ears. "You were way ahead of them, girl."

"Auntie Lily!" Two little voices now cried in unison. "Auntie Lily."

Lily stood up straight with a smile. "I guess our little models are ready for their shoot."

"I hope you mean the flowers," Cade said. "Because those little girls are just that, little girls, and certainly not models."

LILY BLINKED A MOMENT. "I've photographed them before to promote the communal garden. I already mentioned their faces won't be recognizable. And Gina said it was alright."

"Sure. Fine." He made a dismissive hand gesture.

Lily turned away in a hurry. Good she had the flower photo session to focus on, right now, so she couldn't quiz herself about what on earth she had done wrong to make him so hostile. One moment the atmosphere was relaxed and the next it was charged as if with lightning. It seemed Cade…didn't trust her purposes in being here? Did he feel like she was using them? Using the storm damage even, for her own ends?

Gina said it was okay, she repeated to herself. *Now, get on with it.*

With her camera in hand, she'd feel more secure, as if it was a shield to hide behind. To show him she was a professional, doing a job. Cade's opinion about her didn't matter. If he disliked her idea for some reason, he was allowed to. Period.

"You look adorable," she told the twins. Their turquoise rubber boots brought a splash of additional color to their bright yellow dresses. "Now I need a large basket to fill with flowers. You have to be able to carry it between you. Is there something like that around?"

"How about this?" Mrs. Williams's voice came from behind her and there she was, already holding out the perfect basket: oval, twined, rustic.

"Okay, great. Can you give the basket to the girls? I'll get my camera."

She half crawled into the car's back seat to get the camera bag. She felt like staying hidden inside for much longer than she needed, just to sort out her feelings. She didn't want to feel like Cade's opinion of her mattered. Still it did. If she did get her project here, she'd have to work with him.

And how could she work with someone she didn't see eye to eye with?

The twins' laughter filled the air, mixed with Cade's deeper tones. When she popped up, they were at the back of the car piling flowers into the basket. "Put the flower heads all in the same direction," Cade instructed the girls, "so Lily can get them into her shot."

Her name sounded different when he said it. He drew out the syllables a little, giving it an almost musical ring.

She walked over. "There can be a few flowers sticking out like this." Quickly she rearranged several purple dahlias on top. "It has to look a little unruly or it feels too composed. We don't want it to look like we put too much thought into it. It must feel spontaneous."

Cade straightened up, retracting his hand as if burned. "I see. I have no idea about these things."

"Not a criticism," she rushed to say, "just a helpful pointer." Her cheeks turned even hotter and she laughed uncomfortably. "Go figure. I'm the one telling you to give the donkeys a little space when you lead them so they can figure it out for themselves and here I go, bossing you about."

He tilted his head, holding her gaze. A frown formed over his eyes and she just knew she had put her foot in it somehow. He asked, "Did you just...compare me to a donkey?"

CHAPTER FOUR

"NO, OF COURSE NOT," Lily rushed to say. Her cheeks were on fire. "I…" But there was no way she could explain this that would make it any better. "Girls, this way…" She shepherded her nieces to a spot in the yard where the ground was littered with pink petals. "If you stand like that… That's right. Now hold the basket between you. Perfect! I'm going to take photos. Keep standing like that."

She stepped back and sank to her haunches, holding up the camera. "There we go. One… I love it! Now turn your heads just a little to each other. Hold it right there. You're so pretty! One more. Okay." With every click of the camera her confidence grew. She knew how to do this. During her years at the pizzeria she had made food pics for the restaurant and updated the social media channels. That proven experience had convinced the company she now worked for to give her a chance as a maternity cover. She could also show the Williamses that she was good at what she did.

Stacey turned her head to her. "You never sent the photo of Mollie and Millie. You promised to send it and we'd make it into a poster."

Lily clenched the camera. She had promised, fully intending to follow through. But right after that carefree afternoon with their rescues Barry had died and…she hadn't wanted to look at those particular photos. It hurt too much to see their happy faces, blissfully unaware of the disaster that was about to strike.

She forced a smile. "I'll look up the photo and then we can have a poster made. Okay?" She shouldn't avoid the pain anymore.

Stacey nodded and Ann cheered. Lily said, "Just two more photos and I'm done. Could you stand a little to the left? That's great. Hold it now…"

She was aware of Cade hovering nearby, but when she got up to have a look at the results on the camera's little screen, he was nowhere in sight. Of course he had things to do on the ranch.

Mrs. Williams came down the porch. "Can I see the photos? You almost look like a professional. You put them through their paces as if they were on a real shoot."

"It was always fun to do at the garden and those photos were used to promote on-line and in the newspaper." As she said it, a thought struck her. "Would you mind if a photo of the girls landed in the local news-paper? I could send them a news item. Call it a picture of hope after the storm."

Mrs. Williams smiled at her. "That sounds beautiful. After such a dark night full of worry we can use a little hope. Do ask Gina what she thinks though."

"Of course. I wouldn't dream of decid-ing anything involving the girls without her permission. Where is she?"

"In her room. I'll show it to you. Come along, girls." They all went inside and through a corridor into the ranch's right-hand wing. Mrs. Williams knocked at a door. When a reply came, she gestured for Lily to go inside. She said to the twins, "We'll go find some vegetables for the lunch, girls." The twins ran off bickering about what they should choose.

Lily opened the door and walked into a big bedroom with a double bed against one wall and a beautiful carved-wood dressing table opposite. Gina stood at the window. She turned to her, quickly wiping at her face. "Are you done with the girls already?"

"Yes, they have so much talent. I wanted to show you the shots and ask if it's okay to send some to a local news site. To have them post it with a heading of *Hope after the storm* or something. It can cheer people up and be a good promotion for the ranch. If you're okay with mentioning the name and address people might come here to buy the broken flowers. They can still bring in money that way."

"What a great plan. I know Cade worked so hard for those flowers. Planting new varieties and all. I just can't believe one storm swept it all away." Gina's features contorted. "It's like bad luck keeps following us wherever we go. When will it stop?"

Lily rushed over and hugged her. "Don't say that. It will all be alright. I promise you. I'm here now to help out. You know what we did when the pizzeria wasn't doing well? We took photos of all the dishes and we put them online and we thought up fun ways to attract attention and to promote ourselves."

"The pizza key chains," Gina said. Her voice was strangled with tears but also carried a hint of a smile. "Everyone wanted to have one."

"We'll also think of things we can do here. Let me get it all started. An item in the media, people coming here to buy the flowers and it will snowball from there. I guarantee you."

"I know I can rely on you." Gina stood up straighter and smiled at her. "I'm sorry I keep crying. It's the pregnancy and all the sleepless nights."

Lily nodded. She was happy to accept those excuses. Anything not to have to mention Barry and also dissolve in a puddle of tears. "Now you must help me select the cutest photos. You're the proud mother."

They stood over the camera side by side, going through the shots and selecting two.

Then Lily said, "Why don't you lie down for a while? I'll work on getting this sent out."

Gina gave her a watery smile. "Thanks, Lily. You're the best."

Lily quickly left the room and shut the door. The best? She felt like a fraud. How would Gina feel if she knew the full truth?

She hurried down the corridor back into the big kitchen. She had to get online and put the photos out into the world.

CADE HAD RETREATED into the orchard to pick up the pieces there. Remove the fallen apples, give the tree that had toppled a support. Being busy like that, with his favorite thing in life, restored some peace in the turmoil inside. The chaos caused by the appearance of that whirlwind woman.

Part of him admired Lily for her easy manners, how she had stepped into their lives and acted so naturally as if she had been here before. With her friendly demeanor and charming way to present an idea she had completely won over his mother. Gina had of course already been her friend. He was the only one seeing trouble on the horizon.

But he wasn't about to let her get to him. If she wanted to snap a photo of the girls and share it on her pages, she could. If Gina didn't mind, why would he get worked up about it? It would probably get a few likes and that was it. Nothing substantial. He considered that whole engagement thing fake anyway so it didn't amount to anything in his book.

While he was working, he thought he heard car engines in the distance. Closer than would be expected if they just passed by on the road. But he didn't really pay attention to it. There was a lot to do and the phone in his pocket kept pinging with new messages from farmer friends who shared photos of their damages and asked for help repairing them. There were a lot of problems to solve and not enough hands to get to it. This was a serious issue that needed to be addressed by a wider group of people. Perhaps he could use his access to a bigger network via the farmers' association to enlist extra help?

When Cade came into the yard, carrying

his overfull jute bag, he stopped and stared. Several cars were parked there. More vehicles lined the driveway. People milled around a long table covered with plastic and holding the flowers Lily had picked off the ground earlier. She stood among the people and was listening to an elderly lady who pointed out flowers to her. Lily quickly formed her choices into a bouquet and handed it to her, while Cade's mother accepted money from a couple, apparently for another bouquet. While he stood there, staring, he realized that Lily was actually selling his flowers. The flowers that were splattered with mud because of the rain. He had told her that they couldn't be sold that way as they weren't a quality product anymore.

Anger rushed through him. How could she do this without asking his opinion first?

No, actually he had already given her his opinion, saying they couldn't be sold, and she had gone ahead and done it anyway. How on earth had she gotten all of these people over here?

He dropped the jute bag against the barn and marched over to the table. A woman was just enthusing that she loved those little colorful rings in the flowers. "They are called collarette," Lily chirped, beaming from head to toe.

Cade stopped dead in his tracks. There were just too many people around now to confront her. It would be painful and harmful to the ranch's image. That was what he was concerned about, not about how she'd feel if he'd shoot down her plan. No, this was purely a business consideration.

He gritted his teeth and turned away.

"Oh, Cade!" Mrs. Jenkins, owner of nearby Heartmont's general store, waved at him as she pushed her way through the crowd. "What a lovely photo of the girls. People are so devastated by the storm damage. You should have seen Main Street this morning. The flowerpots we hung on all the lampposts to give the street a more inviting look? All broken." She tutted. "And some businesses lost their signs. They were flung through other people's windows. It's one big mess. I admit I shed a little tear looking at it." She gave a firm supportive nod. "But then my husband showed me the website of the *Heartmont Herald* and I saw your lovely photo. They have a live feed about the storm and it was all sad images until this one."

"Photo?" Cade echoed, confused.

Mrs. Jenkins pulled out her rose-colored phone. "My daughter gave me this when she bought a new one," she explained. "Young people, they have a new phone every few months. Mine was a fossil, really. Without internet. She insisted I needed this, so we can message each other. Took me a bit to find my way around it." She shoved her glasses higher up her nose and studied the screen. "Oh yes…" She pushed a few buttons. "There it is. I saved a screenshot of it to look at it over and over."

She held out the phone. The entire screen was filled with a shot of Stacey and Ann seen from behind while carrying a huge twined basket with flowers. The ground under their feet was muddy with trodden pink petals. A few words formed a caption in bold pink lettering. *Hope after the storm.*

Gooseflesh formed on Cade's arms. Here were his sister's children, having lost their father and their home, having ended up on a ranch that was struck by the first derecho in thirty years. They carried a basket brimming with broken flowers and still they were a symbol of hope. Because life went on. Because there was always sunshine after the rain.

"Isn't it pretty?" Mrs. Jenkins said. "The small article with the photo mentioned you were selling off all the flowers today before they wilt and as the store is closed anyway because the window needs fixing, it made sense to come out here and grab some before they sell out."

"Sell out?" he repeated hoarsely, still not over the shock of seeing Gina's children in that photo, representing both sadness and joy, loss and survival.

"Yes, judging by the inpour of people..." Mrs. Jenkins gestured to the driveway where new arrivals were tumbling from cars and rushing to come see the offer. It was a chaos, but a happy one. There was excited chatter, laughter... People were glad to step out of the mess made by the storm and come here. Come together.

Mrs. Jenkins put her phone back in her pocket. "Thanks for doing this," she said.

"You already do so much for others and then this. We all appreciate it."

Before Cade could say this hadn't been his idea, she was off, marching away in her rubber boots to find her car.

Cade returned his gaze to the table with the flowers. He wanted to see Lily. Wanted to study her as she was working and wonder how on earth she did it. How she touched people's hearts and made them smile.

He would never have agreed to this idea. He would have thought it was pointless and even impossible. But she had simply gone ahead and done it. And it worked out so well. For the ranch. For the community.

But where was she? He didn't see her at the table. His mother was serving people and there was Gina also lending a hand and chatting to a woman with a baby in a stroller. But no Lily anywhere. Had she gone inside to get something? Scissors, paper, tape, whatever she might need?

He was also going in. Supposedly to wash his hands. But if he ran into her, he'd say he was surprised by the turnout. That people seemed to be enjoying themselves. That…it had been a good idea.

Nothing too exuberant. That would sound fake anyway, coming from his mouth. But a compliment of sorts. She did deserve it.

He walked inside, rolling up his sleeves higher, so he could wash a little dirt off his lower arms. He entered the kitchen area.

Lily stood at the sink. Her back was turned on him. She was probably busy with something.

"Hey," he said walking up to her. "A real crowd out there. I must say I was surprised. People have a lot on their mind on a day like this and…" He halted beside her and glanced at her, his hand already reaching to open the tap. But it froze midair. Lily wasn't busy with something. She stood there, very still, looking very pale. In the sudden silence he could hear her labored breathing.

"Are you alright?" he asked. Instinctively he reached out for her, but stopped himself before he actually touched her.

She jerked her head up, giving him a startled wide-eyed look. "Yeah, fine."

Sure. You don't look fine. "Maybe you should eat something," he said. "You've been on your feet for hours."

"It's not that." She turned away from him, ambling to the leather club chair and running her hand across the back. "I was just... I don't know."

She sounded a little lost. Cade stared at her back. In situations like this, he never knew what to do. How to act. Get closer, ask questions. Or simply allow her space and say nothing.

He opened the tap and put his hands under the running water. It felt good to have the cold rush over his skin. He focused on it so he wouldn't to have to think of her and how vulnerable she had looked standing there. If he did think about it, he would probably have to say or do something and he had no idea what the right thing would be.

If there even was a right thing.

LILY WAITED FOR Cade to fire questions at her. Are you okay? Do you need to sit down? Is it crowds that get to you? Here's a glass of water...

But although she heard water running, there was no offer of anything. He didn't speak. He just rummaged around behind her. He was there but without forcing himself or his solutions on to her. It felt surprisingly good.

She didn't want to hear everything would be alright.

Because it wouldn't.

It had hit her all of a sudden as she had stood in the yard surrounded by so many people. The person who mattered most to Gina and the twins wouldn't be coming. Barry wouldn't jump from a car and rush to hug his girls, smile at Gina, wrap an arm around her and hold her close. He was dead and he'd never be back with them.

The enormity of it had struck her like a bucket of ice-cold water. Whether she sold flowers or did a million other things to help Gina, it made no difference anymore. Her friend, her sister-in-law who was like a real sister, had lost her husband and her future. That hurt. That would continue to hurt. It couldn't be erased by well-meaning actions or... What had she been thinking when she had decided she had to sell those flowers?

"There's no need to explain yourself," Cade said softly. "We all need a few moments to ourselves every now and then. Especially on a day like today."

She turned and looked up at him. There was a smudge on his forehead as if he had rubbed it with a dirty hand while he was working in the orchard. Merely wiping sweat away? Or was he also standing there looking about him and wondering how he was going to restore all of this damage? He was a strong able man, and she didn't doubt he knew everything there was to know about the business he ran here, but when a storm swept in like that and destroyed so much, even he had to feel like he couldn't fight it. That not even the deepest determination in the world would help any.

Cade smiled at her. A reluctant slow smile that took its time lifting the corners of his mouth. But his eyes also warmed and that feeling reached out to her gently as if to say it was okay that she had nothing to say because she didn't have to say anything right now.

"Good turnout," he said, gesturing over his shoulder. "Mrs. Jenkins, of the mercantile, showed me the photo. You sent it to the newspaper, right?"

"Yes. I did ask Gina and your mother how they felt about it. I didn't want to invite a crowd here if they didn't want it." She eyed him with a frown. "Should I have asked you? Are you in charge really?"

Cade made a soft sound almost like a huff. "Technically I am in charge, yeah. The ranch is mine after my father passed away. But my mother still decides lots of things around the house and big business decisions are always talked about. If she is dead set against a thing I want, I won't force it on her. But she gives me a lot of space to make decisions about the ranching side of things as I have a lot of experience with it." He shrugged. "I don't think you should have asked me about a photo of the girls. That is more Gina's call to make. Besides, obviously I know too little about this promotion thing. If you had asked me whether an action like that would have any result, pull in any people, I would have told you no. They're all busy with their own cleanup—they have no time to come over. And look at the yard now." He walked over to the window and looked out. "They're happy to be together, to chat and feel connected, especially on this difficult day. They aren't all locals either. I heard several people talking who are tourists just passing through. They checked the local websites to learn more about lasting storm damage to roads etcetera. They only wanted practical information on the live feed coverage but the photo touched them and they decided to drop by and do their part in supporting the restoration of the community. Isn't that wonderful?"

Lily felt a rush of excitement at the idea that she had really touched a chord here.

"I asked them to put their names and email addresses on a list and they did. All of them did. I had sixty addresses already when I went inside and your mother and Gina will also ask people."

"Addresses?" He had a question mark written all over his face. "Why would you need their email addresses:?"

"For the At Home on the Ranch newsletter?" She forced a wide smile as her heart pounded painfully in her chest. "I mentioned earlier how you could engage people by sharing a little about your life on the ranch. It was an impromptu idea to ask for the email addresses on the spot but the thought behind it is solid. You see, you have people coming to the ranch now. They like what they see. They want to be involved. This is an excellent opportunity to get their contact information so you can be in touch with them again. Otherwise you let them drive off and they are gone forever."

Cade stared at her. "You mentioned it earlier, yeah, but I didn't really catch on back then and I'm not following now. What newsletter?"

"At Home on the Ranch. I thought it had a nice catchy ring to it. You can share about the work on the ranch, the animals. Funny stories, cute photos. And a call to action at the end. Buy the apple cake. Support the pet rescue."

"What apple cake? What pet rescue?"

"All the pets Gina brought here have been rescued. They now live here and have a wonderful life. A new home. You can ask people to support them, cover the costs of stabling and feeding them. Maybe people can even adopt them, sort of. Become a patron of a donkey or a guinea pig. You could also do that for your cows."

"My cows are not rescues."

"I know that. But you could ask people to become a ranch patron. That entitles them to exclusive news and…once a year, the big Day on the Ranch."

Cade's eyes widened. "Day on the Ranch? You mean, I actually have to invite these people over here?"

"It's no big deal. There are people here now. They look around. They buy flowers. You can add apple products. Cake, cider, whatever. Or maybe towels with embroidered apples on them. Rustic mugs with a ranch theme. A fun motto or slogan that people love to showcase on their desks at work. Then other people see it and want to know more about it."

Cade raised a hand. "How did we get…" He spoke slowly and distinctly as if he was trying to follow a very difficult math problem. "From an email address on a list to a coffee mug with a ranch slogan on someone's desk that is meant to bring even more people to this Day on the Ranch thing?"

"That is the best part about promotion. The possibilities are endless. It's all about selling yourself every way you can. You can keep it small or go all out. You can build it over time. Start with one initiative and add others. According to the time and money you want to put into it."

Cade raised a hand and covered his eyes. "Lily, this could very well be because this seems to be the longest day ever, but... I really don't want to sell myself."

"Well, not yourself as in your own person, but what you do here. What you achieve." She tried a winning smile. "Aren't you proud of it? Don't you want to tell the whole world about it?"

"No. Yes. I mean, I am proud of it, but I don't need the whole world to know. I have contacts. I make a living. There is some damage now but if we're frugal, we can save up and repair everything over time."

"But you don't have to wait. You can do a fundraiser and get together a big amount of money quickly."

"I don't go asking people for money."

"You won't be asking for money. You

can offer something in exchange. Something unique."

"Like a towel with embroidered apples on it?" Cade headed for the door. "Look, Lily, I appreciate what you are doing now, selling the flowers that wouldn't have brought in much otherwise, but just…leave all the rest to me, okay? I think I know what I'm doing." He disappeared and she heard the door shut. Not with a bang. Still she suspected he was angry. He felt like she'd butted in and made decisions he didn't agree with. Not even the successful sale of the flowers could fix that.

She took a deep, steadying breath. This wasn't the way to get Cade enthusiastic about her promotional plans for the ranch. Instead of jumping him with all her great ideas she should have asked him what he thought might work and then developed from there. But she had a feeling Cade might have said he didn't think anything would work, or needed to, as things were going just fine.

Well, she'd just have to try some other time. Catch him at a better moment and convince him her ideas were worth a chance. After all, her dream job in Denver depended on it.

CHAPTER FIVE

"So what do you think?" Cade asked as he wiped the tea towel across the last dinner plate. Gina and Lily had left to take the girls to bed. They were exhausted after the long day. Lily had promised them a story but Cade doubted they'd be able to keep their eyes open until the end.

"About what?" his mother asked. She was washing a very greasy pan.

"Lily." Cade took a deep breath before adding, "She does her best to blend in, I guess."

"You make it sound like she shouldn't."

"No, that's not it. Only... Come on, we all know she's used to a far different life in the city. She has no idea about the challenges of the countryside. She thinks she can apply the ideas that work for her firm's clients one-on-one to our situation."

"Oh yes, she was actually really surprised we had an internet connection. I think she had expected to be cut off during her stay here."

"She does have internet on her phone," Cade countered and then saw his mother's cheeky grin. "You're pulling my leg."

"You're asking for it. You're the one treating Lily as if she landed from another planet. Oh no, an alien popped up in my flower field. She has no idea how people live here. Let me tell her."

His mother grew serious in a heartbeat. "Or rather, let me not tell her but just let her feel through my silence that I don't like her and don't want her here so she will leave again as soon as possible."

Cade grimaced. "I tried until she told me about the embroidered tea towels."

"What?"

He related how he had complimented Lily on her success in pulling people over to buy the flowers until she had sprung the entire newsletter, patrons, Day on the Ranch thing on him. His mother listened without comment until he was through concluding with a terse, "I'm so busy already I don't need her loading new commitments on me."

"But you also do the newsletter for the farmers' association."

"I write some parts of it. I don't actually format it and send it."

"But you know the person who does. They can tell you how to do it. You could think about it."

"Newsletters never get read."

"Then why do you write articles for the farmers' association one?"

"Because I have to. They asked me two years ago and…"

"You've kept doing it ever since." His mother flung down the dish mop and put her hands on her hips. "That's the trouble with you, Cade. You take on commitments and then you keep on ploughing like a horse with blinders on. You don't evaluate if it works or…"

"It's not my newsletter. They should evaluate it. And I'm sure they do."

"Have you ever heard anything about any evaluation?"

"No, but…" Cade shuffled his feet. "Are we done with the dishes? I have some calls to return."

"Not so quick." His mother eyed him earnestly. "Lily has some very good ideas. In any case, she has the expertise to give us a few pointers. And she wants to do it for free."

"Wrong." Cade held her gaze. "She wants to do it because it can get her a permanent position at that marketing firm where she has the temp job. We are her rural flair ace card."

His mother burst out laughing. "Oh, Cade, you make it sound like a crime. Lily only wants to kill two birds with a single stone. It sounds like a very practical idea to me. And you should be glad. You never want to accept anything for free. No charity, that's your motto. She gets something in return that she wants. That is our payment to her. No charity, no strings attached. You should be happy."

I don't feel happy. Cade reached up and pressed his index finger to his forehead. He really had to think about this. "Do you see us selling embroidered tea towels?"

"I do see us sending out a newsletter. All you need is a few photos of the animals and the land… Lily offered to help with that. She is a good photographer. She can do a few shoots and then you have a ton of pictures to use in the future. She can also give you pointers on what to write about."

"Thanks, Ma, but I know what to write about." Cade put the tea towel on the sink. "You can manage cleaning up those few last bits. I do need to return those calls before it is too late. Everyone had a hard day and will be looking forward to falling into bed early."

"Once Lily is back from putting the twins to bed and telling them their favorite story, you could show her around a bit. Tell her the things she needs to know for the project."

"We haven't even decided yet whether there is going to be a project." Cade turned away from her and then turned back as swiftly. "Or have you promised her it's a go?"

His mother spread her hands in an apologetic gesture. "Lily has been on her feet all day to collect the flowers, get them ready, sell them... She made great bouquets, had the brilliant idea to gather contact information to stay in touch, the girls obviously adore her..."

His mother closed in on him. "Cade," she said, her voice falling, "you know how Gina struggles to show the girls a happy face every day. She can't do it all on her own. Let Lily help her. They have been the best of friends ever since Gina met Barry. She asked Lily to organize the wedding, the honeymoon. Lily also helped out when the twins arrived, and with the pizzeria. They have been so close. Gina needs her. A friend her own age she can confide in."

"She has you to talk to."

"I'm her mother, not a friend. Look, Cade, Gina moved out years ago. She lived her own life. She came back here because she had to, but that doesn't mean that she is suddenly a teen again who has to follow my rules because she's staying under my roof. She is an adult with her own life. I treat her like that."

"And I should too?"

"I didn't say that."

"But you meant it. You think I'm patronizing her."

"That sounds so negative. You want to protect her. And that's understandable. But you must give her some room to figure things out for herself. She has a lot of responsibility now. For the twins and the unborn baby."

"Then she should let us help her with that. There's no need to do it all alone."

"You must give her space, Cade. She'll talk about things in her own time. Or maybe never. But we can't make her talk to us."

"And you think she will talk to Lily? We have to take her in hoping she can get through to Gina?"

Cade wanted to say more but a change in his mother's expression made him look to the kitchen entryway. Lily stood there. She said hurriedly, "Gina is sitting with the girls for a bit to make sure they don't wake up again and discover they're alone. She thinks they're still a bit spooked from the storm. I uh... I'd better turn in as well."

She vanished quickly, her head down.

His mother gave him an angry look. "She overheard what you said."

"I wasn't saying anything negative."

"No, you only made it sound like she's the last person in the world Gina should actually confide in. Go after her and apologize."

"That will only make it worse."

LILY HURRIED TO the guest room allotted to her. When Gina had said she wanted to sit with the girls for a bit, Lily had already been reluctant to join Mrs. Williams and Cade in the kitchen. He had made it clear he didn't like her ideas for the ranch and she almost felt like he didn't want her here at all. She had tried to convince herself that she was overreacting but having overheard his words...

It had sounded as if he hated her for actually wanting to get close to Gina again. He had to blame her for something. Or just her family. Barry, her parents, all of them.

"Lily!" Footfalls sounded behind her. "Listen. Uh..." The awkward silence spoke volumes. "Do you want to see the orchard? I mean, we run an apple ranch and you haven't even seen our pride and joy. The trees."

Lily stood with her hand on the doorknob. She wanted to say she was super tired and they could do it some other time. She really wasn't in the mood to walk beside him sensing he resented her being here.

But if she fled into her room and lay on the bed staring at the ceiling, she'd be thinking about him anyway. Speculating why he disliked her so much and felt obliged to shoot down all her ideas. Maybe if she accepted his offer and joined him for the tour of the orchard, she could learn more about him and his views. Maybe she'd discover he was just a thick country hick and she didn't need to care for his opinion at all...

She turned and said, "Sure. It's too early to turn in anyway. And I don't like to watch a lot of mindless television."

"Really? I always imagined it like that in the city, every window of the fifteen-story apartment building giving the same view— a sole person sitting on the couch with a microwave meal in their lap flipping past too many commercial channels."

She wanted to tell him that he really had a lot of outdated prejudices when she caught the twinkle in his eye. "You're kidding me, right?"

"Of course. I have to take full advantage of your city girl image. Although you really surprised me with your rubber boots. Better put those on again. Those..." He gestured at the white sneakers she had slipped into before dinner. "Would soon be ruined beyond repair."

"One moment." She ducked into her room and put the boots back on. The temperature was still warm and clammy, so she didn't need a cardigan or anything. "There we are." She followed him outside. "Too bad about the broken stained glass."

"I'll have it fixed."

"Nice design with the apple tree spreading its branches. We could use it for your logo."

"Logo?"

"Yes, you need a brand logo to put on your website, in your newsletter header and on labels you can attach to your products."

"No apple cakes and tea towels please."

"You need a logo." she insisted. "For the sign along the road too. This morning when I drove out here, I could barely find you."

"You're not a local. If you live here, it's self-evident."

"If we want to reach beyond your existing audience, we need to make you more visible. Literally." She glanced at him. "These days people love for brands to have a face attached to them. So they can connect with the person behind the brand. You are perfect. You look exactly like one imagines a rancher."

The remark seemed to make him stiffen. "So before you ever knew any ranchers, you pictured them to look just like me?"

A treacherous blush crept up. She hadn't actually been dreaming about ranchers before Barry had met Gina and told them his girlfriend was a rancher's daughter, but she had always had this image in her head of the handsome lone cowboy and that was Cade to a tee.

She said hurriedly, "Would you want to be part of the branding or not?"

Cade laughed softly. "Here we go again. Before long you will be saying that I need to sell myself. But I'm simply a guy who milks cows and grows apples."

"And people are fascinated by that. You have a story to tell, an authentic true life story. You can talk about the generations who came before you. How they built the ranch house and made the land suitable for an orchard. How they lived and what they sacrificed. Those stories have appeal and can make people feel sympathetic toward your cause."

"So I have to tell stories of hardship to sell stuff? It's not my thing."

"Everyone has a story to tell. There are elements in it that are more or less sellable. We have to look for those elements. You want to pull people in. It need not be terribly personal. It could also be a...family tradition. A special local custom. Something we can build on."

She glanced at him. "Your brand consists of your core values. So what would those be?"

"Loyalty, community, hard work." He shrugged. "About any rancher here would give you the same reply."

"So we need something a little more specific. Something that is unique to you and your ranch. You did step into it after your father died."

"Don't drag my father's death into selling stuff." Cade's voice held a warning tone.

"I'm sorry. I didn't mean to..."

She wanted to explain better, but he was already saying, "My father died in the orchard. Should I invite journalists over to see the place where it happened? Tell some sob story to earn a few bucks? No thanks. If that is your idea of helping us, then just forget about it." He lengthened his stride and got ahead of her.

She stopped at the entry to the orchard, not sure if she should go after him or see this as her dismissal. He could be so bull-headed. Could she even discuss anything with him?

Then again, he had sounded genuinely angry talking about his father. He had mis-understood and…

"Cade!" She rushed after him. "I don't mean that you have to tell the story that way. You don't have to…use your grief for gain. That's how you feel, right? But I never meant it that way."

"Look, Lily…" Cade halted and put his hands up in the air. "You and I are just poles apart. We have absolutely nothing in common. How can we work together to promote the ranch? We can't."

She expected him to walk on after this as it sounded pretty final. But he remained standing looking at her as if he waited for her to…disarm his arguments?

"I can't claim we have an awful lot in common," she said with difficulty. "But there is one thing we both want."

Cade held her gaze. "And what is that?" he asked slowly.

She had to swallow before she could get it out. "We want Gina and the kids to be happy."

CADE STARED INTO the chocolate eyes of the woman who confounded him on all counts. Who was she; what did she want here? Why did she have to make everything that was already incredibly complicated even more so? He didn't need this kind of headache.

"We do," he agreed. "But I'm afraid we have very different views on how to make them happy."

"Really? I just want them to have a home. A roof over their heads and food on the table. When they were on the brink of losing everything, I was desperate for them to have a safe place to go to. I couldn't take them into my small apartment. I didn't even have a spare bedroom. Look at what you offer them here. Their own part of the house, plenty of space for the girls to play.

They got to keep their beloved animals. This is exactly the safe haven I wanted for them. You must keep offering that. But you need support after the storm. Now, I have two options for you. Number one—I open a fundraising page online and I will shamelessly beg perfect strangers to put money into your ranch…"

Cade felt everything inside him protest against this option. There was no way he was going to let strangers pay his bills.

Strangers who felt sorry for him, at that!

"What's number two?" he asked.

"I make a plan for how you can attract more tourists to the ranch and use it as a pitch to stay on at the firm where I work. You get marketing tips that would normally cost you thousands and I get a shot at turning the temp job into a permanent one. I've always wanted to work in marketing. It requires business skills and creativity—you have to tailor every campaign to the customer's needs. Never a dull moment. And I have a great apartment in Denver now. I love my colleagues at the firm where I work. When I get that permanent position, I get bonuses for every successful project, a company car, all the benefits. After all that happened this year, I need stability and perspective. I don't want to move again, or have to resume job hunting. So when you agree to this, you're not just helping Gina and the twins, your mother, the entire community, but also doing me a favor. What do you say?"

Cade looked into her eyes. After all she had done for Gina and the twins, he wanted her to have a chance at the dream she was pursuing. Maybe he couldn't understand the appeal of it, but people had to do what they loved. That gave them energy and made life worthwhile. Besides, if he didn't agree, she'd make good on that threat to open a fundraising campaign online. Ma and Gina would have no objections and he'd be stuck with donated money he didn't want. He had to take the other option.

She reached out her hand to him. "Deal?"

Cade waited a few more heartbeats. Standing here in the orchard that had been his family's for generations he sensed the importance of making the right choice. Of not being too proud to accept help...no, he'd rather call it input when he needed it.

He took her hand in his. "Deal."

They looked into each other's eyes.

Cade said, "But how are we going to work together? We just agreed we have nothing in common. I mean, we might want to make Gina happy but...how can we ever get results if we don't see eye to eye about anything?"

"It might not be so bad." Lily retracted her hand. "I can scratch the embroidered tea towels. And we need not focus all of it around something we randomly pull out of a top hat. There must be something ready-made, some local thing, we can connect with and that we can properly dress up for our purpose."

"I don't really follow," Cade had to admit.

"Like I won't follow when you discuss agricultural terms. But as long as we are both good at our own end of things, we can make it work." She eyed him. "When I say I'll do something, I mean it. I'm true to my word."

"Me too."

"Then nothing can go wrong. Come on." She walked away, leaning down to pick up an apple he had missed.

Cade looked at her back. She had just said it in so many words. Nothing could go wrong. Why then did he have a sinking feeling that he was going to regret this?

CHAPTER SIX

THE NEXT MORNING Lily was up and about early to answer some emails for work. A colleague asked for her input on a slogan he was working on which had to contain certain words. She tore a few sheets of letter-size paper from her work book and wrote the words on them in big letters. She then put them on the floor to look at them and hopefully have a brilliant brain wave as to how they could best be combined.

When nothing struck her, she decided she needed a change of scenery and took the sheets into the kitchen. The scent of fresh coffee was in the air and she found the pot on a warmer. She poured herself a mug and savored the mocha taste as she studied the words which were now spread across the kitchen table. Slogans shouldn't be too long and should be easy to remember. So she couldn't add words at liberty or make the slogan too difficult. Word play was good as long as it was obvious. If you had to explain it, it didn't work.

She walked around the table with her coffee, reciting the words slowly. *Fresh, innovative.* Man, those were so general. They could fit about a hundred brands. Why hadn't they been more specific in naming their core values or the essence of their business?

"Good morning." Cade breezed into the room. He wore a checkered shirt with stonewashed jeans and cowboy boots. The smile on his face suggested he had seen some of her brainstorming antics.

Lily flushed. "Good morning to you too. Working already?"

"Like you." Cade went to the fridge and opened it. "I'm cooking some breakfast. Want some?"

She saw he'd taken out milk and eggs. "You can cook? Excellent."

"Well, if you call making pancakes cooking." He opened the cupboard to get flour and a bowl.

"Oh, I love pancakes. I'll let you know what my star rating is."

"Fine, as long as you don't post them to social media."

He produced a whisk from a drawer and set about creating batter. Lily watched his tense shoulders with a frown. "What is your gripe against social media? I had a look at the farmers' association website and they have social media." She had also seen Cade's photo flash by. He had been reelected as regional representative. She had stared for a few moments at his determined jawline and earnest gaze. She understood why people trusted him to stand up for their interests. He looked…capable. Reliable too. Someone you could have faith in.

Too bad he was so difficult to work with.

"Sure, and when the association uses them, they come in very handy. They can ask members for a quick vote on a hot topic or share news. I just don't like it when people let their meal go cold because they have to photograph it for some post." He shrugged. "But if you want to let my pancakes lose flavor for likes, it's up to you."

"I won't do anything of the kind," she assured him. "Besides, I'm working." She gestured at the sheets. "I may be out here scouting my pitch project, but I still have my regular work to do."

"I see. So you don't have to be in Denver, physically, to work there?"

"Not all of the time. I do have to show my face in the office every now and then. It's not like I can hang out with my parents in Florida and work from there."

"They still have the resort?"

"They do." Lily grabbed a sheet and started to write down pointless slogans just for distraction. She really didn't want to talk about her parents' resort. When they had first bought it, and renovated it to become the luxury destination they had envisioned, all had been well. But later problems had cropped up with roofing and permits were denied for new activities and it had all become a major headache. And one of the reasons why, when Barry had died and the debts came to light, they hadn't been able to jump in with any financial support for Gina and the girls.

"Do you see them often?" he asked.

"Not often. Just for a holiday or birthday, you know. But my mother calls every now and then. To ask how I'm doing." Lily stared at the last few words she had written with a panicky urge to come up with some topic, any topic, to get him away from the current one. When she'd given him all the reasons why she had to turn the temp job into a permanent position, she hadn't mentioned her parents' expectations. They had been very disappointed and hurt over the loss of the pizzeria, in which they had invested so much time, energy and money when it had still been theirs. Dad had said she could have found out sooner Barry was making a mess of finances. That he had believed the pizzeria would do well because she was there to keep an eye on Barry. It had made her feel like she had failed. And she so wanted her parents to be proud of her. "That smells good."

"They always say the first one is just for tryout. I'll eat the tryout one." Cade slipped the pancake from the pan onto a plate and put new butter into the pan. While he let it slide so it covered all of the bottom, he asked, "Do you want anything on yours? Raisins, apple? Bacon, cheese?"

"I usually have two with sweet toppings and then two with savory."

"Okay. What would you like for sweet?" Cade carefully lifted the tryout pancake with his fingers and took a bite. He chewed and then gave her an elated smile. "Not bad for a start."

"Apple, please. We're in apple country after all."

"Sure." He grabbed one from the fruit bowl and washed it under the tap. The relationship between Lily and her parents intrigued him. Just a phone call every now and then to ask how she was doing, nothing more? "Do your parents ever come to see you? I mean, have they been to your place in Denver?"

"No, but they're busy at the resort. It has forty-two cabins near the beach and they recently added glamping tents."

"Glamping tents?" he echoed, never having heard the term.

"Yes, it's like camping but with running water, bathroom facilities and a real bed with a soft feather mattress."

"So what is still camping about it? I thought the charm of camping was having to do without your usual comfort."

"People like the idea of being outdoors. But they still want a level of…luxury. They're on holiday after all."

"I see. And your parents cater to that kind of crowd?" Did it also mean Lily loved luxury? When extolling the virtues of her job in Denver, she had mentioned bonuses, a company car and so on.

"Well, it makes sense. The Keys are a hot tourist destination so there are enough potential customers there. But it's also teeming with hotels, camping spots, inns and hostels so to attract customers they have to stand out. You can do that in various ways. Be cheap. Be special, like uh…spending the night in an old lighthouse. Or you can go luxury. Everything has to be just right. The decor, the food, the activities offered at the resort and the information about what you can do in the area."

"Has to be perfect, huh?" Cade asked, mentally gritting his teeth. Here he was in his stable clothes, making pancakes for a woman who came from a family serving lobster and caviar to the in crowd at some Floridian beach resort.

He got another plate and slipped her pancake onto it. He carried it to the table and put the plate down, casting a cursory look across her sheets. "Just one word per sheet?" he queried, with a hitched brow.

"I can shuffle them around. I'm brain-storming a slogan."

Fresh, innovative… Was she also thinking of using those words to describe the ranch? Where had she gotten that idea? Or was it more that the ranch had to become like that? His back tightened at the idea of having to change just because they were going to involve people, tourists who had to like it. Before you knew it, Lily might decide that red and white were the ranch colors and everything around the house had to become red and white so the tourists coming in could feast their eyes on what they considered country living. He suddenly had a mental image of country line dancing in his yard, a man playing terribly on an old fiddle and tourists clapping along while a woman dressed as a cowgirl served pints of beer.

"Maybe we should reconsider," he said, returning to his pan.

"What?"

"Working together. I don't know if we have the same ideas."

"About what?"

"The ranch."

"Do we have to?"

"Don't we have to?" He threw her a puzzled look. "I mean, you may want to promote it as fresh and innovative while I want to keep doing things like my grandfather did them and you think the tourists won't notice?"

Lily stared at him, then burst out laughing. "These—" she gestured at the sheets "—are only meant to give feedback to a colleague of mine. They have absolutely nothing to do with the ranch."

"Oh…" He rubbed his neck.

"Although you do have innovation here. What about the new dahlia varieties? You try new things."

"Sure, but…it's not like reinventing the wheel."

"You don't have to." Lily smiled at him. "In fact, instead of trying to be ahead of the pack all of the time you can also just do what you do best and do it better than anyone else. That is convincing to people because it carries authenticity. I think an environment like this—" she gestured around her "—will sooner evoke a picture of being firmly rooted in the past than jumping on every new bandwagon."

"Is that good or bad?" he asked. "I mean, in your book?"

She held his gaze. "Professionally or personally?"

He didn't know what to say. Her personal opinion shouldn't matter to him, maybe, but she wasn't just a marketing expert breezing by. She had a shared past with them. Her family had become Gina's family through marriage and… Of course it mattered. In a family you needed shared values. Things you believed in. Common ground to stand on.

"I smell pancakes!" Ann came running into the kitchen. She was in her pajamas and clutched a doll to her chest. She rushed to Cade and asked if the next one could be for her. Cade looked at the pan and saw the pancake had burnt during his conversation with Lily.

"This one is a little overdone, sweetheart,"

he said to Ann. "I'll make a new one, okay? You go and sit with…"

"Auntie Lily." Ann turned her back on him and made for Lily showing her the doll and saying something about new dolls' clothes for it.

"Oh yes, I see," Lily said. "A new blue dress with crowns. Is she a princess now?"

Ann leaned into her. "We saw the fabric at the farmers' market. I asked Gran if she could make my doll a dress out of it. And she did. I also have a dress for myself. Shall I put it on?"

Without waiting for the answer she rushed off.

Cade shook his head. "I'll give this pancake to you then when it's ready." He checked his watch. "It's a little early for her to be out of bed anyway. I was surprised to find you here."

"I'm a morning person." Lily stretched her arms. "I do my best work when it's still quiet. That's perfect here. I stood at my bedroom window and I didn't hear a thing. No traffic, no sirens. Not even birdsong."

"Oh, if you had waited five minutes, you would have heard our rooster. He's awfully loud and insistent." He came over to bring her the pancake. "So how many stars do I get?"

LILY LOOKED UP into Cade's blue eyes. They held a hint of amusement, but they also still struck her as aloof. He had immediately assumed she was sitting here pinning words on his ranch that he didn't think fit. They might have struck a deal last night, but that didn't mean there was a truce or they were seeing eye to eye.

Far from it, it seemed.

"I can't judge yet. Let me have that one and then the savory. I need to form a better opinion of your skills."

Cade seemed to sense that she meant more than just the pancakes. He returned to the stove.

"You can also make one for yourself in between," she said. "After all, I assume you came in for breakfast. What have you been doing already?"

"Milking cows. That's about the first thing I have to do in the morning."

"Oh, does the milk truck come to collect it and then take it to some factory where they make cheese out of it? I saw in a documentary on TV how that works."

"No, we make our own cheese. It's a small enterprise, but my mother loves it."

"How wonderful. That is a nice authentic touch we can address in the newsletter." Lily tilted her head as she studied Cade. "We do need to get on that. People have been here, they have the flowers in their vase, they remember the ranch with a smile. We have to follow up on that momentum. I guess then…" She angled for an empty sheet. "First thing we need is that logo for the ranch. To use in our header. I was thinking…" She posed her pen on the paper and chewed her lower lip. "Something with a tree or trees?" She drew a basic tree shape with a trunk and an oval canopy above to represent the foliage. She might add a few apples to it. Hmmm, it was a bit simple maybe…

She started anew, doing separate branches. That was harder since her talent for drawing wasn't award winning. Not a stellar result. Then maybe… "What do you call the ranch?" she asked. "Does it have a special name? Like Big W or something?"

Cade laughed. "We're not in a Western movie. It's just the Williams place to people around here."

"Hmmm." Lily wrote *Williams* in capital lettering and then had branches extend from the *W* and the *S* with two apples on each. "How about this?"

Cade came over and looked at it. He shrugged. "Yeah, I guess."

"That doesn't sound very enthusiastic."

He lifted a hand. "Look, I have the roofer coming over for the barn. Turns out I couldn't fix it myself. There is a long list of people who all have damage to repair but he offered to come to me first because he still owes me a favor and I can lend him a hand so it won't take too long and he can quickly get to the next job. That's my priority now and I really don't have the time or the inclination to discuss some logo for some newsletter…"

"That you don't want in the first place." Lily leaned back against the chair. "Cade, I understand that you feel that your priority should be with the practical matters— repairing damage, caring for your animals and your trees. But if this plan of mine is a success, it can deliver money in the long run. You also have to look ahead. Plan for the future. You can't just go by the day."

Outside a car horn honked. "That'll be the roofer." Cade gestured at the stove. "Can you finish making pancakes for the twins? I bet that Ann ran back to get dressed. Stacey will pop up here too, in a minute." He looked at her papers on the table. "Ask Ma about the logo. Or Gina. They can probably be of more help to you than I can."

He left the kitchen and she heard the outer door close. It annoyed her that he placed himself outside the negotiations about how the promotion for the ranch should be handled. But on the other hand it might also make it easier. If Mrs. Williams and Gina agreed to her plans, she could press on.

Humming, she stepped up to the stove to make pancakes for the twins.

CADE SAT ON the roof of the barn, waiting until the roofer would tell him to hand him more material or hold the blowtorch for a moment. After a close look at the damages he had said they weren't as bad as could have been, considering the weather, and the leaks were fixable without taking the roof apart. That meant the animals could stay where they were. And the bill would be reasonable. He should be thrilled.

Instead he was thinking about Lily's suggestion of a logo for the ranch. It made sense to have one and her impromptu drawing had impressed him. Not too many frills, a symbol of sturdiness, durability. She did understand what the ranch was about. Even if she was a city girl who had only seen real-life ranching in a documentary on TV.

Maybe that was what rubbed him the wrong way. That it didn't need to have been like that. Lily could have come here sooner, known more about their daily life. After Barry and Gina were married, they had been invited countless times for holidays. Ma had made it clear Barry's parents and Lily were more than welcome too. At the ranch there was always room at the table for guests. There could have been big Thanksgiving meals, Christmas Eves with stories and games and Ma's famous apple pie. But despite the many invitations they had always had an excuse not to come; they had stayed away like the ranch wasn't good enough for them. No wonder. Lily's parents had a luxury resort in Florida. Glamping tents. Camping but with feather beds.

He huffed. He'd never understand it. But apparently she did. She got up early in the morning, not to milk cows or clean out stables, but to work on projects that led to bonuses and a company car. That was her lifestyle. Her world. And to the casual observer it made a lot more sense than ranching where the long hours were paired with the constant uncertainties of fluctuating produce prices and the risks of inclement weather ruining a whole season's work. How could someone who had not grown up in the country ever understand the appeal of it? How a newborn calf stole your heart and there was no better feeling than looking at a freshly harvested crop?

"Almost done," the roofer said. He wiped sweat off his brow with the back of his hand. "You really are lucky, Cade, that I could fit this in. I've got a list as long as my arm to take care of. Not days of work, no, weeks. It will take a while before we have this whole derecho thing put right."

"I appreciate it. I guess you don't have time for coffee when you're done?"

"Nope. I barely have time to breathe." The roofer huffed. "My wife said she'd probably not see me again until Thanksgiving. People have lost their entire barns. Have to be rebuilt from scratch. One woman called me…" He fell silent for a moment, shaking his head. "Husband passed away in the spring. She was crying her heart out. Needs help to rebuild. But has no money. I'd love to help her, but do you know what that costs? I can't afford to offer my services for free. Besides, if I do it for her, I'll have others calling me soon after. There aren't any rich farmers in this district. No one has a ton of money in the bank for this kind of thing." He put his tool in the belt around his hips. "Speaking of the bank, I heard Hanson has been calling people to say, all honey-tongued, he can approve an extra mortgage for them. At steep interest rates."

"That man really can't resist making a buck, can he?" Cade said with bitterness.

"Not even if he has to do it across the backs of storm victims."

"He calls it business, my friend." The roofer carefully lowered himself to get on the ladder that was leaning against the barn. "He always says he runs a bank, not a charity. I guess that we all have to be a little more like him if we want to survive." His dark eyes were earnest as he gazed up at Cade. "I'd love to help that widow, Cade. I honestly would. But I can't. I need to make a living. I have a wife, two kids, bills to pay. I just can't… But it gnaws at me. That woman's tears…" He shook his head as he climbed down.

Cade followed him. When they were on solid ground, his mother came over with a wrapped package in her hand. "Something to eat on the way over to the next job," she said holding it out.

"Oh, thank you, ma'am. That is really nice of you." The roofer accepted the food and said to Cade, "I'll send you a bill."

"Good. Thanks for coming and fixing this so quickly. I really appreciate it."

"We all do," his mother said. "Thanks and see you later."

"Bye." The roofer got into his truck. Sitting in the driver's seat he opened the package and grinned in appreciation. "Chocolate muffins! Still warm," he called through his half-open window. "My favorite. Thanks."

Cade looked at his mother. "I thought you were going to make cheese this morning. Where did you find the time to bake muffins?"

"I didn't. Lily did." His mother eyed him innocently. "She said something about you being awfully busy today?"

Cade felt his neck redden and he quickly turned away from her. "The barn is fixed now, but I'll climb up in the loft to see what needs cleaning up there. Then I'll be in the orchards."

"Don't you want a warm chocolate muffin?" his mother asked with her head tilted. "Or at least a cup of coffee? Normally you run on coffee."

"There's just too much to do." Cade made a dismissive gesture. "The roofer told me that he got a call from a widow who was in tears because her barn collapsed in the storm and she doesn't have the money to rebuild. I have to think up a plan to help her. We can't let one of our own struggle."

"Why don't you ask Lily to help out? She seems to know a lot about fundraising. Did you look in the jar to see how much money we got for those broken flowers? It was a brilliant idea of hers."

"Sure, on a day like yesterday people feel sympathy for the cause and they want to buy a few flowers. But the tourists left again to see the Rockies or whatever else and they no longer think about us. To Lily this is just a project, something to cut her teeth on and win a job with or something. But this is our life." *Our everything. There is nothing else but this. Everything we worked for rolled into this ranch.* He took a deep breath. "I'm off then."

LILY LOOKED OVER her shoulder when Mrs. Williams came into the kitchen. She had first said Lily should offer the muffins to the roofer herself as she had baked them, but Lily had declined saying it was rather awkward as she didn't even know the man. Truth was she hadn't wanted to see Cade and sensed that a few muffins wouldn't help to bridge the gap between their different outlooks on life. Thing was, baking helped when she felt sad or angry. She had baked a ton after Barry had died. Baking things and then sharing them with others, making them smile, was the best way to fix the hurting in your own heart.

"The roofer was really glad to have something to enjoy on his way to the next job. He says thanks." Mrs. Williams walked to the table where the coffee mugs stood ready, alongside the big plate full of muffins. "Cade is too busy to come in."

Apparently Cade didn't see the joys of sharing sweet treats. Lily sighed. It had been worth a try. Even if she should have known that someone like him wouldn't fall for a bribe.

"He really has an awful lot on his plate," Mrs. Williams said.

"Maybe it wouldn't be so much if he knew how to delegate." Lily sat down with a thud.

Mrs. Williams seemed to suppress a smile. "You sound just like me when I was talking to Cade's father. He always wanted to do everything on his own. Build this place, grow the orchard, sell the harvest. I pushed him to forge alliances and hire help, but he always believed that if you want a job done properly, you'd better do it yourself. Cade sure inherited that philosophy." She sat down and grabbed her coffee mug, wrapped her hands around it and sipped with a pensive expression. "He had a lot to deal with when his father died. Cade was only twenty-two at the time. He had graduated college, had plans to settle somewhere with his girlfriend Shelby."

Girlfriend? Lily tried not to perk up at this mention of someone who had actually liked the taciturn cowboy and had envisioned a future with him. *How?*

Mrs. Williams said, "Shelby was a nice girl. I guess it would have worked out if the ranch hadn't come between them. Cade had so much to take care of here and…well, he threw himself into it with gusto. He was always working. Shelby had a job and was here weekends. But even then Cade was working. Not just on our ranch. He was also helping friends with theirs. I guess it was his way to work through his grief. He's not a big talker."

Lily silently huffed. *So I noticed.*

Mrs. Williams stared ahead as she continued, "I was sad when Shelby broke up with Cade. I thought he really needed someone in his life. Someone who tore him away from work and forced him to be social every now and then. But Shelby had met Cade before his father died, when he still had plans to have a normal job and live away from the ranch and... He was always cast as the successor you know, but not so soon. We all thought that Cade would take over when my husband was ready to retire. That would have been about now, had he lived. But he passed away ten years ago and...things were suddenly fast-forwarded. Shelby couldn't keep up with the changes."

"Changes in the life they were going to live, or changes in Cade?" Lily asked.

Mrs. Williams considered for a few moments. "Both I guess. Shelby had met Cade at a time in his life where he was...different I suppose. Away at college he had played football and taken Shelby out on dates, weekends away. When he came back here, there was no time for that anymore. It was all work. Cade got sucked into it and..."

"So it wasn't his choice?"

"I guess that was the issue with Shelby. Cade kept saying he was just having a busy season and it would wind down after that, but it never did. He likes work." She sighed. "Over the years I tried to get him to date. But there aren't many single women in the area, and after Shelby he doesn't want a long-distance relationship, doesn't think it will last. He needs someone who would be willing to give up her own life and move in here. I don't mean overnight of course, but…"

"Didn't he care at all that his girlfriend asked him to cut down on the work and have more time for her?" Lily pretended to be focused on her chocolate muffin but everything inside her was primed to hear the response. This whole situation reminded her painfully of her parents and their dedication to the pizzeria. Her father had felt like he had to keep a close eye on the staff or they'd be slacking. Her mother had wanted to make sure every candle on the table was in exactly the right spot and the napkins were folded the way she liked.

They had lived for their business. It had been their baby.

Maybe more than their own children?

Barry had once said to her, "I wish they had never started it. Now it is always there and... There is just no getting around it."

She bit her lip. Maybe it had been the wrong decision to let Barry take over. It had seemed like such a wonderful thing: he could step into a successful business, his future was ensured. For him and his new family. Gina, the children they'd have... It had made so much sense. Especially considering Barry never really knew what he wanted to do. He had tried various things but always got itchy feet. Stability was what he needed.

But had they judged that right?

Mrs. Williams had thought about her question and now said, "I don't know. Honestly. I could never figure out why it ended between the two of them. I mean, I do know how Shelby felt. She said so, aloud, to anyone who wanted to hear. But Cade never said much. He carried on after she left. That was it."

Lily nodded. She recognized that. Just do

what you have to do. Don't discuss things you can't change anyway. After Barry had died, her parents had never said how they felt. How they coped with their grief now that their son had been so suddenly torn away from them. Had they also experienced that heady mix of emotions that had whirled Lily around in a vortex? Pain, sadness, but also anger because it was so unfair that he had died so young and his children would miss their father?

Had they also felt betrayed by him, because he had incurred debt and the pizzeria had to be sold? Disappointed? Puzzled?

Even guilty because they had been a part of it?

It would have helped so much to talk about it, to simply acknowledge those feelings were there. But as they kept silent, she didn't dare say anything either, afraid she'd hurt them even more by putting her emotions into words. They were her parents, she loved them. She wanted them to feel better, not worse.

"Is there still a muffin left for me?"

Lily froze. Cade had come in anyway. She had wanted him to, but now, right on top of the story about his ex, she wasn't so sure. Mrs. Williams had meant to explain to her how Cade felt the need to always be working, but it was something that didn't resonate at all with her. She now found it even harder to cooperate. On a plan to make this ranch more profitable so he'd have even more work to do? More reasons to hide behind and avoid social contacts and...

Was that even right?

It's none of your business what he does with his life. Whether he has time off or is a workaholic. There are so many people just like him. Forget about it and just do what you have to.

"I'll go and get Gina and the girls," Mrs. Williams said. "They went to have a look at the vegetable garden to see what we can cook for dinner tonight." She left the room.

Lily sipped her coffee wishing it wasn't this quiet on the ranch. She would so appreciate a radio playing loud music now. So loud she couldn't even hear herself think.

"How about this?" Cade said. He reached down and put a piece of wood on the table beside her half-eaten muffin. It was a round piece, a slice from a trunk, with the bark still on it like a ring. Lettering had been burned into the beautiful wood. It formed the name *Williams* with two branches with tiny apples on them, just like she had sketched it this morning. Only it was much better now. The design had come to life, giving it exactly that rustic touch she had been looking for. And there was a direct connection between the name, the brand and the wood.

She looked up at him. "It looks amazing. Where did you get this?"

"I made it." He shrugged. "My dad taught me how to make such wood engravings. If you have a suitable piece of wood and a decent engraver pen, the actual engraving doesn't take long. The iron tip burns the lines into the wood just like you were writing with a felt-tip. The tools were all still in the shed and…"

"But still, you said your to-do list was so long and…"

"This took priority. You see, once you have this, you can get on with your ideas for the ranch. And I do think we need those ideas. Besides, it was fun to do. I used to do it a lot in the past but lately..." He fell silent and shuffled his feet.

She looked at the expert piece of work, her breath catching at its beauty and the details she only noticed upon closer scrutiny. "You should get back to it. You're talented."

"I thought you could photograph this for the newsletter heading and...other places where you might need it." He shrugged again as if it was but a minor thing. "You said you were aiming for an authentic feel, something that is unique to us."

"Yes, and this will work beautifully. Thanks."

Lily looked into his deep blue eyes and there was so much she wanted to say that her brain blocked and nothing would come out. Here he was handing her the perfect logo, so he did understand what she wanted to achieve. It need not be about changing what they stood for, but using what was already there.

"We need the help." He said it slowly as if it was hard to get the words out. "Not just us here on the ranch but this entire area. We need tourists to come and spend money so we can rebuild. The roofer told me a story about a widow crying her heart out because she doesn't have any funds to rebuild her barn. This is about more than us, our survival. About more than Gina and the girls. You came here for them, I know, but…the area needs your ideas. This newsletter, At Home on the Ranch, it shouldn't be just about me, about this ranch and the apple orchards. It should also feature other ranches, other people's products. We have a ranchers' association newsletter but that is agricultural news aimed at ranchers, insider information full of jargon. We need a more accessible insight into our lives and our work, aimed at customers. It should be a stellar advertisement for people to come here and buy and do things. I don't know yet how we can make it work but…we must do something. It's high summer now, tourists are flocking to the Rockies and…we need our piece of the cake. You were right all along and I was wrong."

Lily stared at him. He was coming round in a major way and she should be jumping for joy. Now she could make her project even bigger and have a better chance of securing that permanent position. She could do more work to help more people and have a truly satisfying time here. But he had placed himself outside of the equation in a clever way. It was not about him, his ranch, no, it was about helping the region, all those people in need, the poor crying widow. Deep down inside, she sensed that it was his way of not letting it get close to him. Needing others, needing help. *He* was the one helping, reaching out, making a change.

Was that why he had buried himself in work? So he could do something useful and feel like it mattered?

"You don't seem thrilled," Cade said. He frowned. "I thought you would be happy. You do want to do it, right?" He sounded worried, as if he already saw her backing out of her offer.

"Look, Cade!" Stacey ran in. "It's a giant cucumber. We can slice it up for lunch. And there is more."

Gina followed with a basket holding more cucumbers, red peppers and tomatoes. "We could make a big salad," she suggested.

"Or have veggies with dip," Ann said.

"Lily can show you how to make a tomato basket."

"What's that?" Gina asked pointing at the wood slice on the table.

"The new logo," Lily said. "For the ranch. Cade made it."

"Lily gave me the drawing to work from. It was no big deal. I got a bit dirty on the roof. I'd better go change." And he left the room.

Lily said quickly, "It's not like I bossed him into it. I didn't even know he could make things like that."

"Oh, Cade is full of surprises," Gina said. She stood at the sink. "Are we going to wash these, girls?"

The girls cheered and drew up their stools so they could reach high enough to help prepare the vegetables.

CADE PULLED OFF his boots and threw them on the floor with a thud. "Of all the infuriating people in the world," he muttered to himself, "Lily Roberts must be the worst. One moment she wants me to do something. Show an interest in her logo, make sure it's something very special. The next, once I've done it, it should have been something else. It should have been, apparently, because she wasn't happy when I said she can do her project and benefit everyone. She can go bigger and she's not jumping for joy. I'll never understand her."

He dressed in a fresh shirt and jeans, threw the others in the basket in the bathroom. It stood beside the basin and he caught a glimpse of himself in the mirror. There was a look of frustration in his eyes because he just didn't get her.

At all.

He sighed and leaned on the basin giving himself a long, hard look. "You may not understand her. But you have to stop rubbing her the wrong way. She can help. Not just you, the entire town. She has to get this project up and running, you understand? You can deal with her. Just listen to her ideas, lend a hand. You need not judge her, personally, or her background, or her brother."

Cade clenched the basin. He had struggled with his questions before, but now that Lily was here, they'd become unbearable. She must know all of it. Why Barry had done the things he had, taking irresponsible risks. Why Gina had changed so much and felt too good for her own family, never visiting them anymore. Why the closeness they used to share had been broken and it had felt like he had lost his little sister…

He closed his eyes. *There is no point in asking,* he told himself. *It all happened. Gina is in debt. Barry will never come back. You can't change it, only accept it. Stop thinking about it. It's over. Focus on the here and now. Helping Gina, solving the debts.*

A knock on the door and his mother called. "Cade? Are you in there? We are going to eat some vegetables with dip now. Early lunch and then we can all go on with our work. You joining in?"

"Sure. Just washing up."

Her footfalls faded and he looked at his mirror image again. A determined man who knew what he wanted and usually got it. Logical that the whole frustrating situation with Gina and the debts got to him. He hadn't been able to prevent it and even now, with the remaining debts and the storm damage, it was questionable whether he'd be able to solve it soon. But he had to try.

He splashed water into his face and toweled dry. Then he gave himself one last look.

You can do it.

Just be professional about it.

LILY PRETENDED TO be fully focused on making the tomato baskets when Cade came back in. She cut the top part off the tomatoes, scooped the inside out leaving a hollow basket that could be filled with finely ground red pepper and cream cheese or other fillings. Finally she created a C shape from the top part to make a handle.

"Creative," Cade observed.

His aftershave swirled around her, a spicy scent with hints of vanilla. He carried a plate with cucumber slices to the table and offered to help peel the eggs his mother had boiled. The girls were mixing the dip from yogurt, mayonnaise and fresh herbs.

"Does the garden bring in enough to be self-sufficient?" Lily asked Mrs. Williams.

"In summer we often have too much and

share with neighbors. Or we turn fruit into preserves. In that cupboard there are some delicious strawberry and blackberry jams from last year."

"Great." Lily carried her plate with the tomato baskets to the table. "I thought I could snap some photos this afternoon of life on the ranch. So we could put out a few jars of preserves on a checkered tea towel or something? And I want to do a shoot with the animals."

"Can we be in it too?" Stacey asked.

"If your mother thinks it's okay."

"Just our hands petting a guinea pig," Ann said. "Not our faces."

Gina nodded at Cade. "See? They know how to keep their privacy protected."

Mrs. Williams sliced the bread while Cade peeled the eggs. Then they all sat down to eat. The wood slice with the logo was still on the table. Mrs. Williams said, "It reminds me of the woodwork demonstration your father used to do."

"Oh yes, when we were little," Gina said. "He sat in a booth and people told him what they wanted him to engrave on their wood slice. Names, dates, a special symbol. They watched as he created it. It was a huge success." She frowned. "Wasn't it at some fair or other?"

"Apple Fest," Mrs. Williams said. "It was an annual event presenting the region's produce, with music and crafts. It used to be quite big. There was a couple organizing it. The Cloverdales. They knew everyone and got them involved. When Mrs. Cloverdale died, her husband didn't feel like continuing anymore and it sort of…got forgotten. You often see that with people's pet projects. It's one person or two pulling all the weight and when they can't any longer, it just ends. I wish it hadn't. It was good fun."

"And an excellent way to showcase what the region has to offer." Cade looked at Lily. "You said last night you'd need something to connect your marketing effort with. Something that is already here. A tradition or a local custom."

"Or a past event we can breathe new life into." Lily stared at him. "That sounds brilliant. I assume…" She looked at Mrs. Williams. "That there are photos of past occasions?"

"Sure," Mrs. Williams said, as she got up

and went to the cupboard along the far wall. She opened the lowest door and looked in. She rummaged for a few moments and then came back to the table with a large leather-bound photo album. "They should be in here." She opened the album and leafed through it. "Oh yes. Here's your father doing the wood carving." She passed the album to Cade who glanced at it and smiled. He shoved the album to Lily. "That is typically Dad. The blue overalls and then the tools all cluttered around him."

Lily looked at the man who was an older version of Cade. He sat in a booth at a table littered with tools and wood slivers and worked with a focused expression on two entwined hearts while a young couple stood waiting for him to finish. It was a perfect little scene that could go straight into a country magazine.

"There are more photos of Apple Fest in there," Mrs. Williams said. "You have a look. Go ahead."

Lily turned the page and discovered shots of booths with preserves and ciders. Kids receiving prizes for the pig or calf they cared for. And then a shot of the Williams family: Mr. Williams with his arm wrapped around his wife, Gina a teen in jeans shorts, a younger girl with a straw hat and Cade with a pretty young woman who leaned into him with a confident smile. Shelby? They looked like one big happy family.

Her finger hovered over Cade's then girlfriend, but descended gingerly on the straw hat atop the younger girl as she asked, "Is that April, Gina?"

Gina nodded and Mrs. Williams said, "Funny…back then I could have sworn she loved country life and would always live in this area. But then the travel bug caught her and…" She hesitated a moment and swallowed. "These days we don't see her much."

Lily felt a prick of guilt that her careless request for the album stirred up these emotions. It was as if the awareness of all the loved ones that weren't here anymore hung heavy in the air. Not just April who was alive and well, absent by choice, but also those who had been snatched away: Cade's father, Barry…

Gina said, "I guess you can use some

old photos to show how it used to be. And then we can see if we can do something like it. It was always in October when the full harvest was completed. It was prepared months in advance and I think we should get something up and running sooner to uh…use the momentum you talked about earlier?"

"And raise money to help people rebuild," Mrs. Williams added. Focusing on something practical seemed to distract her from her emotions. "How can we do that with such little time?"

"Well, we need a location," Lily said. "And booths. Items to sell. If there aren't any apples yet…"

"Early varieties can be harvested soon," Cade said, "so we would have some apples. And it wasn't about produce alone. Also about crafts and performances. We can still have those and use them for fundraising."

Lily looked around the table and saw enthusiastic faces at the idea their town tradition could be revived. This was what she had aimed for: to engage them in something they already cared about. It had to come from the heart.

"Okay. Activities. Musicians. Artisans." Lily looked at Cade. "I guess you have contacts enough. Ask around if people would be game for something like that. A day of celebrations about what this area stands for. To raise money to help with the storm damage. Everyone who can contribute somehow should send us an email to say what they can do. And we need to pick a date. Not too far away but not like this week either because people are still cleaning up around their homes."

"How about in three weeks' time on a Saturday?" Cade said. He pulled up his phone and checked the calendar on it. "Second Saturday in August?"

"Perfect," Lily said. "We need a basic schedule ASAP and then we can print some posters and put them in stores and at gas stations, places where people pass through. I'll then make the first At Home on the Ranch newsletter about the revival of Apple Fest. Just a small version this year, in August, but it could become a new annual tradition in October from here on. If you want to."

"Then we'd need a new organizing committee," Gina said. "After Mrs. Cloverdale died, no one was game for it. Why would it be any different now?" She leaned her elbows on the table and gave Cade a worried look. "I mean, as long as you do all the work and they can share in the raised money, people will be enthusiastic. But to get it up and running for real, in the long run…"

"We'll cross that bridge when we come to it," Lily said. Her head was suddenly full of ideas and she was excited to get going. She grabbed her phone and started to make some notes.

Mrs. Williams shook her head. "Look at that. Family lunch and you're both on your phones typing away."

"Just emailing a few friends," Cade said. "To see if the date is workable."

Lily said, "I'll make a list of things we need. The bare essentials."

Mrs. Williams grimaced at Gina, but her eyes were twinkling. Apple Fest was about to be revived.

CHAPTER SEVEN

"So where are we going?" Lily asked Cade as he steered his SUV down a dirt road.

"You'll see. Just a few more minutes."

Lily rolled her eyes, but was secretly also a little excited. He had told her he had a surprise for her and had refused to say any more. Ever since they had thought of reviving Apple Fest, there had been pings on his phone indicating incoming emails and messages and she could now see firsthand that he really knew everyone around here.

The positive responses and offers to help weren't just because of the great idea or the noble cause, but also because people liked Cade and wanted to lend him a hand when he asked. He was good at what he did and that gave him confidence. She wanted to feel that too, do her job and see results, have projects to be proud of. She wanted to prove to her boss who had taken her on without a bachelor's degree or working experience that she needn't regret that. There were colleagues who doubted her skills and who were skeptical about whether she deserved a permanent position. She had to show them that she did.

"There it is." Cade pointed ahead to a ranch house painted in deep red with black accents. "That's my best friend Wayne's place. He grows wheat and corn, has horses and breeds cattle dogs. Rosie comes from one of his litters." He parked the SUV beside a large barn. As he turned the engine off, Lily heard a loud noise. As if someone was cutting down trees with a chainsaw. "What is that?" she asked.

Cade grinned. "That is the surprise." He jumped out of the car and quickly rounded it to open her door for her.

Lily stepped out and looked around her. The place didn't have cheerful hanging baskets or a cute sitting arrangement on the porch. It looked sparse, practical rather than cozy. "I bet your friend is a bachelor. I don't see a female touch around here."

"Right, but don't mention it. It's his touchy point." Cade winked at her. She didn't know if he was serious or not, but she didn't intend to make a faux pas and annoy his best friend.

They went in the direction of the sound. Rounding the barn they came to an open area with a large tree stump. A tree had previously stood there, but it had broken off. A tall dark-haired man was working the stump with a chain saw. But he wasn't cutting it up. He was carefully shaping it.

Lily's mouth almost fell open when she saw what he was doing. How every movement with the seemingly crude chainsaw chiseled away carefully at the wood, giving more detail to the animal that was springing from it. A deer or goat-like creature it seemed.

The man noticed them and turned the chain saw off. He came over and reached out a hand. "Hello there. You must be Lily. Cade told me you had come over to help out after the storm. You're Gina's sister-in-law, right?"

"Right. Pleased to meet you. What are you making?" She nodded in the direction of the stump.

"A mountain goat on a rock. The tree

broke during the storm. It was too bad because it had stood there for over fifty years.
But things like that happen. I thought I'd
make a nice memorial out of the stump.
And I also have plans for the tree itself."
He looked at Cade. "Are you going to tell
her or shall I do it?"

Cade gestured for Lily to come closer
to the wood creation. "I asked Wayne," he
said, "to come to the Apple Fest and create animals out of pieces of wood. People
can watch his demonstration and then at
the end of the day we can auction off the
wood sculptures for the good cause."

"That sounds brilliant."

"There's more. He is also donating the
tree that fell to the festivities. We will cut
it into slices and I will engrave them like
I did for the ranch logo. People can buy a
slice with their names on it, dates that are
important to them… Like Dad did at Apple
Fest earlier. I can't claim to be as good as
he was but…"

"People will be happy to see the old tradition revived," Wayne said. "You should also
ask Mr. Konrad to carve wooden spoons."

"Ma called him and he agreed to come

and bring already-made pieces plus demonstrate his skills on the spot."

"Good. So we have a lot of wood crafting lined up." Wayne rubbed his forehead. "Can I get you a quick drink? It's hot and it sounds like you've been busy."

Cade nodded. "Sure, something cold would be nice."

Wayne nodded and went inside the house. Lily walked around the tree trunk. "It's amazing how large a tree gets in fifty years."

"In the woods you can see trees that are hundreds of years old. Dad used to take us when we were little to find the biggest trees. Tallest or with the largest trunk diameter. We used to stand around them and then try to touch each other's hands. Form a family circle."

"That's nice." Lily smiled as she touched the wood with a finger.

"Did you ever do such things with your mom or dad?"

Lily shook her head. "Not really. My parents put a lot of hours into the pizzeria. It was open seven days a week, so we couldn't get away a lot. They did take us on a big vacation in the summer but... Dad would still be in touch with the person who took over at the restaurant for him. He couldn't let go really."

"But if they were working that much, how was that for you? Were you home alone much?"

"Yeah, most of the time when we came home from school there was no one there. We got ourselves a drink and snack and we did homework or watched TV. Or we went to friends' places. It was a lot more fun there."

Cade gave her a thoughtful look. "I can't imagine that. My parents were always around. I mean they worked here on the ranch, so when we came home from school, there was always someone there. Or they were easy to find. Just go into the orchard and we could talk to them. We could always bring friends and play in the barn or in the hayloft. I've always imagined raising my own kids that way. Making them feel like home is the best place you can be."

"It's not like I disliked being at home. It was just that…it would have been nice if they had more time for us. They worked hard to provide for us, ensure we had the best of everything."

Wayne came back out carrying a tray with glasses of lemonade. "Homemade," he said.

"Really?" Lily accepted a glass and took a sip. "That's delicious. Is it a secret recipe?"

"Not exactly. Fairly easy to make." Wayne lifted his glass to Cade. "To the revival of Apple Fest."

"Apple Fest," Cade echoed and took a sip.

"Oh…" Wayne waited a moment, his lips curling up as if he was thinking of something incredibly funny. "Will it also be the revival of the Heartmont Heroes?"

Lily saw Cade cringe. He almost choked on the lemonade. "What is the Heartmont Heroes?" she asked curiously.

"Wait. I'll show you." Wayne put his glass down on the tray he had set on the ground and ran back to the house.

"Don't," Cade called after him. He took two steps as if to rush and overtake him, then shook his head and took a large draft of lemonade.

"Is it something special?" Lily wanted to know.

"Something best forgotten," Cade said with a grimace.

Wayne came back out, running over with a grin from ear to ear. "Here it is," he cried and shoved a photo into Lily's hand. It was obviously pretty old, with dog-eared corners, and it showed a platform where a band performed. Three young men, one on drums, two playing the guitar. They were also singing judging by their wide-open mouths as they leaned over to microphones.

Wayne said, "May I present to you… the Heartmont Heroes?" He held out his hands and made a gesture as if strumming a guitar.

"Oh, you're one of the guys in the photo?" Lily asked, looking closer.

"Yep. And our other guitar hero is Cade."

Lily did a double take. Yes, now that she knew it was him, she did recognize his features. But his hair was different and… It just wasn't easy to reconcile the sturdy cowboy with the youthful rock star in the making. She suppressed a grin.

"Don't say it," Cade warned her.

Wayne laughed. "Come on, don't be a spoilsport. It would be fun. I bet people would be paying money just to see us play again."

"I haven't touched my guitar in years," Cade said. "I don't think it's a good idea. Unless you want to send people running for the hills."

"Nonsense, we need to practice a little and we're good to go. These things you don't forget." Wayne turned a little more serious. "You said you wanted to raise funds. Not a few hundred but thousands of dollars. That takes some special doing. If we reunite and offer to do a spectacular performance, we can charge extra for it. Or just ask people to make a donation, whatever. I've got a friend who can help with some professional equipment to ensure we sound good."

"He hasn't got the equipment to make sure two guys who can't sing sound good." Cade didn't seem convinced at all. "Besides, our third man, Len, moved away. We can't ask him."

"We don't need him. We'll be a golden duo. Come on, do me a favor."

"I'll think about it." Cade emptied his lemonade glass. "Lily and I should be going. We still have a few more stops to make."

As THEY GOT back into the car, Cade hoped Lily wouldn't say anything about it. Wayne had caught him by surprise with that old photo. They had been three kids thinking they were the next hit machine in country music. They had thought they were really good. But in his memories they had only been really loud. Everyone had probably endured their singing because they had been local kids and they didn't want to say how terrible they really were.

Lily looked out of the window and then began humming "Country Roads."

"Don't," he warned her, but she started singing anyway. She had a nice voice and could even grab the high notes without trouble. "Maybe you should perform," he said.

"Maybe I will if you do it too," she retorted. She smiled at him. "Come on, it could be fun. We pick some country classics and breathe new life into them. When was the last time you played?"

When I was practicing for my song at

Gina's wedding. Before I heard it was going to be a big formal affair and no one wanted a country hick to play the guitar. He clenched his jaw. "Years ago. Look, Lily, Wayne is known for his wacky ideas. Let him play on his own if he wants to. Or why don't you team up with him for a duet?"

"Maybe I will. I'll give him a call about it later." Lily leaned back in the seat. "I think we should use every opportunity to get people to bring their checks to support the good cause."

"Yeah, well, maybe it doesn't matter to you to look silly on a stage because you will be leaving afterward but I have to live here. I don't want to come into the general store and hear Mrs. Jenkins start humming my song to remind me of my terrible performance."

"She seemed like such a nice woman when I talked to her at our flower sale. She wouldn't do that to you."

"Oh she would." He nodded. "How about the booths? Has that man got back to you?"

"Yes, this morning." She pulled up her phone. "He said uh…" She scrolled through some emails. "That he could do it for a small price considering it was for a charitable cause. But those will be just bare booths. Everyone needs to bring their own decorationss to make it look attractive."

"Okay. We have to let people know. They can dig through their attics for something to use."

"We might need a common denominator."

"What?"

"Well, if everyone brings an old blanket from their attic to cover the booth's surface with and put their items on, or do crafts on, it might look a bit…random. I'm arranging for press to come and we do want to have good photos. So we could tell them to bring their own decorations but preferably in a certain color scheme?"

Cade had to admit she was right that having a few basic rules in place would create a better effect. Still he was also a little suspicious. "Press? You mean, someone from the *Heartmont Herald*?"

"And a few other newspapers. Also uh… TV."

"TV?" he echoed.

"Yes. I have a friend who has a friend whose cousin works at a local TV station. They want to come over and do an item on the revival of this long-standing tradition. They want to uh…interview you too. I had wanted to tell you later but… Now that we are discussing it."

Cade glanced at her. "Why me? Why not you? If you got them interested…"

"I'm not local. You are rooted in this tradition. You attended the Fest when you were a child, then when you grew up… You can show some photos of previous years and… You have a genuine story to tell about it. If I do it, it would feel forced. Like a marketing stunt."

"I see." Cade nodded slowly. "Okay, that makes sense. I guess I can do it. I have some experience with interviews via the farmers' association."

"Great. I knew you weren't camera shy."

Her phone pinged and she checked her screen.

"More offers for the fair?" he asked.

"No, this is work. I sent my boss an outline of what I intend to pitch as my project for the permanent position so I have an idea of how she'll like it. At the moment I can still make tweaks to improve." She fell silent as she read, a frown forming between her eyes. Her nose crinkled as it always did when she was concentrating. It looked kind of cute.

"Doesn't she like the idea?" he asked. For a moment his heart sank. If Lily's boss shot down her pitch, would she stop helping them organize Apple Fest? They had the basics set out and he guessed he could continue working out the details on his own, with help from his mother, Gina, Wayne and all the other locals but…it wouldn't be the same. Lily had put all of this in motion. She should be there to make it into a reality.

"Oh, she does like it but…" Lily chewed her lip as she scrolled down her phone, as if she wanted to reread a bit.

"What is wrong?" His heart hammered now. If her boss didn't like it, and told her to find something else, she might be leaving. It suddenly seemed like such a shame if she did. He had thought there was plenty of time but…he could have been wrong. Why had he dragged her out to Wayne's? They could have gone for a drive and ice cream, something fun, to take her away from all the work.

"She's not negative, but she does emphasize that she can only take me on permanently if I show what I've got. The..." Lily gave a huff. "The woman who I am covering for, Eva Bailey, seems to have quite a say in the company and she told the boss that she doesn't like me to coast in."

"Coast in?" Cade repeated to ensure he had heard right. "Like you're not doing any actual work."

"Well, she doesn't like the fact that I only have an associate's degree and no real working experience and... Maybe it's because I'm younger than all of them or because they've been a team for years and I am the new kid on the block. Maybe I just have to prove myself more?"

"But you're working day and night." Cade cast her a worried look. "Last night you were working on that project you have to finish and you're constantly taking calls and then the pitch project on top of that..."

"I knew what I got into when I offered to help you. I can do it." She put away her phone and looked out of the side window.

Her posture clearly stated that the topic was closed and she didn't want to hear any more about it.

Cade pursed his lips. Of course it was none of his business how hard Lily worked. That was her decision to make. She had an important goal ahead, getting that job and...

An icy feeling settled in his stomach. Was everything she asked them to do meant to beef up her project and get her boss's seal of approval? Was she thinking that whatever it took she had to get the project approved and the entire community would just have to jump through hoops to fit her...perfect picture? Was her emphasis on making things look good just the opinion of the professional who wanted them to have the best chance of bringing in loads of money or did it also have a personal element in it? Lily not wanting to feel ashamed of this simple rural community and their amateurish event?

Could he even separate the two? Lily had a personal stake in their Apple Fest looking good. Her job and her future in Denver depended on it.

Wayne's sudden reminder of the Heartmont Heroes brought it all back to him. How he had sat nights on end lovingly strumming his guitar, composing a song for his little sister's wedding. Even shedding a tear because Dad wouldn't be there to see this.

It was his surprise for Gina so he had contacted Barry to ask him when would be the best moment at the after-party to perform it. Barry had simply said that something like that didn't fit in their plans. "We have a certain standard to uphold, you know, for my dad's business relations and our friends." He hadn't even said sorry.

Cade clenched the wheel. He had wanted to call Gina and discuss it with her, ensure that she at least knew he had proposed the idea. But it would have put her in a difficult position having to choose between supporting her husband-to-be's views or going against them. Cade had thought it better not to force her in a tight spot. Because he loved her.

But right now he wondered if he had done it because he had been afraid. Afraid that Gina would also explain to him that

things were different now that she was marrying into a family who had certain expectations of her. She had said it before when
she had shown them the engagement ring
with a huge diamond in it or photos of luxury trips Barry took her on. That it was
normal in his family and that she just had
to go along with it. That it was nice to be
pampered and visit places she had never
been before. Cade had wanted her to have
that, to feel loved and provided for. But it
had been too much, and it had gone spec-
tacularly wrong.

Cade parked the SUV by the side of the
road and got out. He walked to the fence
behind which a few cows grazed and stared
at the horizon. He just couldn't make sense
of it. Any of it.

LILY HAD LOOKED up when the car stopped.
Where were they? Was this their next stop?
But there wasn't a house in sight.

She got out and frowned at Cade who
stood at the fence. Was there something special to see there? The cows maybe? After
her surprise at Wayne doing that amazing

chainsaw woodwork she could expect any-thing.

She walked up to him. "Is this another surprise? I know nothing about cows so if you expect me to see something special about them…"

"Nope." His voice sounded gruff. "There's nothing special about cows. Or about apple trees and orchards for that matter. Or country folk. No wonder your boss doesn't believe in your project. You should have jetted to New York or maybe Dubai even. When is it far enough away to be exciting?"

Lily blinked. She wasn't sure she followed along. "My boss does believe in it. She wants me to have that opportunity. But I have to convince the entire team. That's understandable. We have to work together in the future and how can they respect me if they feel I was hired for anything less than my great work?"

Cade said, "In that case I can understand if you want to do another project. Something more exciting. More in your league?"

"*My* league? What is my league?" Lily's confusion increased. Apparently the email from her boss had rubbed him the wrong way. She shouldn't have shared it with him. It was never smart to show doubts or… weakness. When would she get that? She had to look capable, in charge. She had to earn the respect of her co-workers and the approval of her parents. It would mean so much to make them proud.

"I don't know. You tell me. You just mentioned your boss wants more from this project. But I don't see how we can deliver. You just said it's not okay for people to drag an old blanket out of the attic to build a booth. Okay, I get you want a better look. In an ideal scenario we should have covers made. All the same color and with a pattern you like. Only too bad we don't have the money for it, because getting some money was the whole point to begin with. I loved the idea of reviving Apple Fest. I really thought it could work. But now… I'm no longer sure our goals are aligned." He turned to her and gave her an honest questioning look. "All we want is some money to rebuild our lives. We don't need perfection. Do you?"

Lily froze. Truth was, she wasn't sure. The pressure was on with Eva Bailey's criticism and suggestions to the others that

Lily didn't deserve this chance to stay. That she had to prove herself worthy of it. She wanted to secure this job. Failure wasn't an option.

For her *and* the community.

"Cade…" Lily stared into his eyes that seemed to search deep inside her for the truth. "Our goals are aligned. I only try to give you tips to make the fair look better. People don't need to buy things for it. I only want to coordinate their choices a little. If it's a hotchpotch it would be a shame…"

"Would you feel ashamed?"

"I would be disappointed because we could have done better. Look, I told you, honestly, that I'm using this project for work. I need something really good, something exceptional. And you need the money it brings in. Now I think Apple Fest has all the right ingredients to make it work for both of us. And it isn't something I drummed up—it's your own tradition. But you have to let me do my job. You have to take my advice to make simple but effective improvements. The press coverage is very important, for both of us. Can't we make it a win-win situation?"

"Yes probably." Cade raked his fingers through his hair. "I'm sorry. Wayne's mention of the Heartmont Heroes brought back a lot of memories. How things used to be and how they changed. And not everything changes for the better. Sometimes you look back and you wonder how did it all happen? And why didn't I do anything about it? Was I a coward? Thinking too much about my own feelings instead of doing what needed to be done."

Lily wasn't quite sure how to respond but Cade didn't seem to expect her to. He said, "Look, I need to check on my ranch hand who is fixing the fencing on the other side of this field. Can you take the SUV back to the ranch?" He held out the key to her.

She accepted it hesitantly. "Are you going on foot?"

"Yes, I need to clear my head. I uh… I hope you're not mad about our…difference of opinion. I do need your help to get things sorted, for Gina and the twins, the town. I would hate to ruin it for them by my behavior."

"Maybe you think too much that it all depends on you." Why had he called himself a coward? She would call him many things—prejudiced, pigheaded—but a coward? No, that didn't seem to fit. He had struck her from the get-go as someone who faced trouble head-on. So what was eating him? "Even if I were mad at you, I'm not leaving. I have work to do here." *On my project and on you. To get you to open up a little, so you see you don't have to do everything alone.*

Cade held her determined gaze a moment and nodded. "Good."

Lily almost had to laugh. She wondered if he'd think it was so good if he knew her thoughts.

CHAPTER EIGHT

"WHERE DID CADE say he was going?" Mrs. Williams asked. They had just finished dinner and she was clearing away the plates. Gina had taken the girls to get ready for bed.

Lily shrugged. "He had to check on his ranch hand who was repairing fences. I had the impression it wasn't a major thing."

Mrs. Williams sighed. "Cade hired Jeb Mahoney because his father asked him to give the boy a chance. He loves ranch work and is a really hard worker, but he has a lot to learn. I guess Cade should have said no as he needs a ranch hand who can work on his own so it actually saves him time. Now he has to check up on Jeb several times a day…" She shook her head. "But Cade believes it will get better."

Lily picked up the tea towel to help with the dishes. "We were at the house of his friend Wayne and he teased Cade about a band they used to have. The Heartmont Heroes? Cade seemed different after that. Like he…didn't want to be reminded." Lily twisted the tea towel in her hands. "I uh… wonder if it was such a good idea to dive into Apple Fest. I mean, you must all have lots of memories of it when… Cade's dad was still alive. Maybe it's painful for him to think of happier days?"

"We were happy then for sure. But his father died ten years ago. I can't imagine…" Mrs. Williams stared ahead with a frown. "Of course I don't really know how Cade feels. He won't tell me." She gave Lily a sad smile. "He's like his father. The two of them were very close. Now when I say that, you probably imagine they talked a lot. But they didn't. They worked together all the time before Cade left for college and during college holidays and that connected them. They were of one mind about the ranch, the orchards, everything. His death was a shock, and I wished Cade hadn't been forced to step into his shoes so soon. When he was still so young. It's the same with Gina now. Being a widow at her age, having two young children and a third on

the way…" She shook her head. "I sometimes can't understand it. But we have to
make do. You don't have to worry about
Cade though. He's good for his word. He
said he'd help you and he will. No matter
what's troubling him now."

*But I wish I knew what it was. That he
would talk about it. Talking is so much
better than silence. If I had only talked
to Barry before he died…* Mrs. Williams
didn't need to tell her how men reasoned.
Barry had been like that. Always a smile,
a pat on her head. "Don't worry, sis, it'll
be alright. I know what I'm doing." And
she had believed him. She had wanted to
believe him. Because she loved him and
couldn't imagine he would do anything to
hurt his family, or their parents' legacy.
He had known how much the restaurant
meant to them. How much time and energy
they had invested in it. Their life blood.
And still he had gambled it away with his
reckless spending. She had believed his
lies that everything would be alright, had
even loaned him money. She had nothing
left to go back to college, get her bachelor's degree. Mom and Dad were push-

ing for that, not knowing the funds were gone. She didn't want to tell them that either, renew the pain over Barry's behavior. She had to make them proud of her. And she could without a bachelor's degree. If only the project worked out.

She swallowed hard. "I'd better go see if Gina needs help tucking the girls into bed."

"Lily."

She halted on her way out. "Yes?"

"Don't take Cade's behavior personally. He may be a loner, but he's got a good heart."

Lily nodded briefly and went into the corridor that led to the guest rooms. She didn't feel like explaining to Mrs. Williams how damaging it could be to accept the stereotype of the strong man who doesn't need help. After all, her cooperation with Cade was a purely professional thing, and a lot rode on making it succeed, both for Gina and the twins, as well as Lily's own future in Denver, the success she craved to build her self-confidence. She wouldn't let anything ruin that for her.

She briefly knocked on the door and when Gina called she could come in, she put her head round the door and asked, "Anyone want cuddles?"

"Me, me," Stacey called and Ann who had already crawled under the duvet nodded, clutching her teddy to her cheek.

Lily came in and looked at Gina. Her face was pale and there were shadows under her eyes. She produced a wan smile. "The baby is really restless today." She rubbed a hand over her stomach.

"Why don't you go and sit down? I can tell the girls a story and wait until they're asleep."

"You sure? You've been working from dawn."

"That's a gross exaggeration. I never get up before seven." Lily conveniently left out that she had already been answering emails from bed. "Now you go and sit. Your mother has some wonderful walnut cookies you can try."

Gina's smile was more heartfelt. "Thanks, Lily, you're a gem." She left the room.

"Does the baby hurt Mommy?" Ann asked. "She says he kicks her."

"Well, suppose Stacey and you slept in a single bed. Then when Stacey turned over, she might just kick her leg against yours and you'd feel that. But it doesn't mean Stacey wants to hurt you. There's just limited space, you see."

Ann nodded with a relieved smile. "Can you tell the story of the princess who traveled the world?"

"Sure." It was one of their favorites which she had told dozens of times. She made slight variations every time so there'd still be surprises. With a smile she began, "Once upon a time in a kingdom far, far away a little princess was looking out of the window. It was raining again. It had rained most every day for a month now. She couldn't play outside. She had done every puzzle and every game she knew. She was bored. She wanted the rain to stop..."

While Lily spun her story about the princess and the discovery of a secret door that led to other countries where it was sunny and hot all the time, Stacey's eyes fell closed. She softly snored while she lay fully relaxed. But Ann's hands kept clutching her teddy and her eyes stayed wide open, dark in her narrow face.

Suddenly she said in a low voice, "When is Daddy going to come back?"

Lily froze. Gina had explained to the girls that their father had died and that he would never be coming back home. They had seemed to understand. Did this question mean that they didn't? Gina wasn't here now to intervene. What should she say?

"He said he would come back soon. Before he left. And on the phone. He said he'd come back and bring us presents. But he didn't."

"Not because he didn't want to, Ann." Lily leaned over to the little girl. "He meant it when he made that promise to you." Barry had always meant it. He had been an impulsive guy and he had made mistakes, but he had genuinely loved his family. He had been madly in love with Gina; he had been devoted to his little girls. But life was about more than feelings. It was about taking responsibility for the promises you made, even when it got hard.

Ann said, "I want Daddy."

Lily bit her lip. Tears burned behind her eyes, but she couldn't show them to the grieving little girl. "I know, sweetheart. And if Daddy could come back to you, he would. But he can't. The snow fell all over him and then he was gone."

"Did it hurt?" Ann asked with huge eyes.

"No. It went really fast. He didn't see it coming. Like when it suddenly starts to rain and you get all wet."

"But then you don't die."

"No, honey." Lily wished with all of her heart Gina was here now to take over. On the other hand, she wanted to save her tired sister-in-law these hard questions and the painful answers. "But snow is heavier than water. It covers a person and then…" *They can't breathe*. She couldn't say that.

"Do they freeze? Doesn't that hurt? Stacey held an ice cube to my knee once and it hurt."

"Because it happens so fast, it doesn't hurt." Lily reached out and brushed a lock of hair away from Ann's face. "Do you worry about that when you're in bed at night? That Daddy was hurting when he died?"

Ann nodded. "Mommy is crying all the time. She thinks we don't know it but I do.

I think she's crying because Daddy hurt himself when he died."

"She's crying because she wants Daddy to come back to you and he can't."

"No, she doesn't." Ann shook her head violently. "When I said it, she told me not to say that. I don't think she wants him to come back."

"Oh, honey…" Lily pulled the little girl into her arms. She wanted to hold her close and make her feel safe, but that way she could also hide the tears that ran down her own cheeks. "Mommy misses Daddy just as much as you do. But she doesn't want you to be sad. That's why she said not to talk about it. But you can always talk about Daddy if you want to. You can talk to me or to your grandma. And to Mommy too. She just doesn't want you to cry and feel bad."

"I will always feel bad." Ann's voice was resigned. "Daddy can't come back so we will never be happy again."

"That's how you feel now. Because it happened a short while ago. But over time…" Lily fell silent. Who was she kidding here? Would it get easier? Would it not matter anymore? These girls would have to grow up without a father. Barry would never be there as they learned how to cycle without his help, as they celebrated birthdays, graduated high school, married, had their own kids. There would always be an empty space. A hole in their hearts.

"I don't want to forget him," Ann said smothered against her shoulder.

"You don't have to forget him, honey. You can always think of him."

"But Mommy said not to talk about it. And it makes her so sad. But I don't want to forget him."

Lily clutched the girl tighter. Poor thing. She had thought that she had to forget her daddy because remembering him brought tears to everyone's eyes. She herself was barely keeping it together. But that was what grief was about. Feeling something. Because that person you lost had meant the world to you.

"Listen now, Ann," Lily whispered, "you can always talk about Daddy. And maybe it makes Mommy sad and you too. But that is alright. It's alright to be sad and to cry. That's part of life. Just like being happy and laughing and having fun. Daddy would want us to remember him. But he would also want us to continue living and doing things we love and having fun together. You can be sure of that."

Ann rubbed her head against her. "I love you, Auntie Lily."

"And I love you."

Lily held Ann until she felt her body relax. She gently lowered her into the pillows and watched her face as she lay sleeping. The tears on her cheeks were drying up. Lily hoped she had said the right thing. Her head was so full of thoughts it could almost burst.

As soon as she was certain both girls slept soundly, she left the room and then the house. She stood outside taking a few deep breaths of the evening air. Then she went into the barn and looked in on Millie and Mollie. They stood close together apparently already dozing. But when she drew near, Mollie woke up and came to greet her, pushing her soft snout against Lily's hand.

"Hey, girl," she said softly. "How are you? Are you happy here on the ranch? You have a far bigger barn now than you used to. And more animal friends." She waited a few moments and then added, "Still I wish we were back home and everything was as it used to be. That the restaurant was still there and... Barry." Her voice caught on his name. She realized how often he was in her thoughts and apparently also in the kids' but nobody spoke his name out loud. As if they were afraid to say it.

Afraid it would break their hearts all over again?

"We don't say it," she said to Mollie. "We don't mention it because that way, maybe we can pretend it never happened. That the restaurant wasn't sold off. And Barry never...died."

As she spoke the word, it was as if a judge's gavel fell. A bang and it was all final. Irrevocable. He was dead. He had been buried under a ton of snow and his life had evaporated in moments. He had probably not noticed a thing. That was the only consolation.

Something creaked behind her and she turned in a jerk. Cade stood there at the foot of the ladder to the hayloft. He gave her an apologetic look. "I was up there," he said, his voice hoarse, "to check whether the leaks are really fixed. I didn't mean to uh…listen in on your conversation."

"A conversation with a donkey?" She tried to sound light and amused, but it didn't really work out. She wondered if he could see the traces of tears on her face.

"Sometimes animals are the best to talk to. They listen, they don't judge and they never disagree with you."

A slight smile tugged at the corners of her mouth. "I bet the last is most important to you."

Cade looked away, letting his gaze travel the barn. "When my father died, I wasn't here. I was at college. I got a call and…it just seemed surreal. I had never expected him to die so young. He was a big strong man. Someone who exuded health and power and energy. Who loved life, who was always doing physical labor. I guess I had believed he'd live to be a hundred. And then he was gone. I came home and…the first few days I was here, doing chores and then when footfalls came, I turned my head thinking it was him. I knew he was dead and still when I was distracted for half an hour, it was like I had forgotten because I kept thinking he'd step into the barn or come around the next tree in the orchard. I wanted him to. Because we never got a chance to say goodbye."

He looked at her. "I guess it's the same with you and Barry. When he had that skiing accident, you could never…"

Lily felt Mollie's soft muzzle brush her arm and she patted the donkey. She was glad for the distraction. Her grief was a lot messier than he assumed. It wasn't just about someone being torn away unexpectedly. It was coupled with so much guilt and regret, and a sense of having failed her parents, Gina and the twins, by not having prevented the disaster. Instead of lending Barry all her savings so he could "work things out" as he had promised her, she should have made sure he got help from a debt counselor or something, whether he wanted it or not. She had believed family loyalty meant covering things up so no one knew of his problems but that had been a huge mistake.

"I'm sorry that we've had such a rocky start," Cade said softly. The scent of his aftershave swirled round her as he came to stand closer. "And that I said we have absolutely nothing in common. I shouldn't have said all the things I did. There's a lot of pressure to make everything work out and... Just forget about it, okay?"

"Not if you meant it." Lily looked up at him. The last thing she wanted was Cade keeping his mouth shut for fear of hurting her feelings. "You don't have to keep silent because you feel sorry for me. Just say what you think."

CADE STARED INTO her eyes. Her lashes were wet. She had been crying. Over her brother, his sudden death, this whole miserable situation. Maybe because she felt powerless to change anything about it. He often felt that way. He understood. He wanted to tell her that. Not that they were different, but how alike they were. At the heart of things.

He reached out his hand and brushed his fingers over her cheek. Her eyes widened a fraction. As if she was surprised that he could be so tender? But that was what she needed right now. Tenderness. Not more empty words about understanding or not understanding each other. That wasn't the most important thing. He wanted to let her know he was here for her. To talk to. To lean into.

He carefully wrapped an arm around her. She leaned into his shoulder. They stood like that, not saying a word, just breathing the hay scent and the quiet of the barn. The animals made soft sounds around them. Overhead new rain splattered on the roof. But they were inside where it was warm and cozy. Nothing could touch them here.

Then a cheery melody filled the room. It broke them apart. Cade stepped away hurriedly with almost a guilty feeling as if he had been caught red-handed.

He fished his phone from his pocket and checked the screen. "It's Wayne," he said, taking the call. "Hello?"

"Hey, is this the new Keith Urban speaking? Can we switch to video calling? I want to show you something."

"Sure." Cade tapped the screen a few times. "There. What do you have to show me?"

Cade could now see Wayne's face on the phone's screen. He stood in a room with a slanting roof so he had to keep his head down not to hit it on the rafters. "I found my guitar. Look. It's as good as new."

"That's great news," Lily said.

"Is Lily there too?" Wayne asked. "I hoped for that. Hey, wait." Wayne apparently put the phone down because the view suddenly showed wooden boards. From farther away his voice sounded. "Let's see if I still remember." A guitar began to play. And Wayne's deep melodious voice sang along.

Lily's expression changed from interested to appreciative. "Wow, he's really good," she told Cade. He grimaced. Wayne was so cheating. No way he had picked up that guitar and started playing. If the thing had been lying about for years, it had to be tuned first. This was a setup to impress Lily.

And it seemed to work. She was listening with all her attention, tapping her foot along to the rhythm. Wayne ended on a dramatic finale and asked, "What do you think?"

"It's fabulous," Lily enthused.

"Do you want to perform with me at the Apple Fest?"

"Uh, well, I'm sure I'm not half as good as you are."

"No problem, we can practice. Come over to my place tomorrow night? Seven o'clock?"

"I can't," Cade said. "I've got a ranchers' association meeting."

"We'll do fine without you, right, Lily? I'll make new lemonade."

"Okay why not? But you might be sorry you ever asked me."

"I don't think so. See you later." Wayne disconnected.

"Is he always like that?" Lily asked. "I mean he doesn't waste any time getting to the point."

"I guess," Cade said. He felt a bit superfluous standing there. He could point out to Lily that Wayne had contrived the whole bit about finding the guitar, but it might sound piqued and childish on his part. If those two hit it off, well, why not? Wayne was a nice guy and...

He shook his head. It was none of his business. "I have work to do." He stepped back. "You will be alright?"

"Sure. I... It was just something one of

the girls said. It made me a little emotional. But I'm better now. I'd better uh…go listen to some songs to prepare for tomorrow."

Lily left the barn. It suddenly seemed very empty. Cade stood tensing and relaxing his hands, not knowing quite how to handle the stillness. He should be getting on with work, but his mind was empty. He could only think he had wanted to say more to Lily, more meaningful things, and now she was gone. The chance was gone.

He lifted his head and shook himself as if to get rid of the thoughts. He always found it hard to put his innermost thoughts into words. He had no trouble talking about tractors or the prices of livestock, but as soon as it strayed into the territory of personal stuff…

Might be better, he tried to tell himself. *It seems like Wayne's call really cheered her up. You should be glad for that. It was heart-wrenching to see her so sad. Wayne's wackiness will make her smile again, laugh even. A brilliant distraction, right?*

Still, it felt as if the distraction should have come from him. He could have offered to take her out for ice cream. A little downtime, away from all the organizing she did. But wouldn't such an invitation be odd, coming out of the blue? He'd need some reason to suggest it or it might be mistaken for...a date? And it definitely wasn't. Their relationship was purely professional and he intended to keep it that way.

CHAPTER NINE

"I'VE SENT YOU my list of recommendations," Lily said to her colleague Pat. "It's just small things. Overall, it looks fab."

"Thanks, Lily, you're the best. I don't know who would have made time for me on such short notice."

"Look uh…" Lily wanted to ask if Pat could put a good word in for her with the boss to pave the way for her project, but she felt awkward asking. If Pat appreciated her presence in the company, she could say so of her own accord, right?

"Yes?" Pat asked.

"Nothing. Let me know if you need anything more done. I'm happy to help. Have a nice day." Lily disconnected and blew a lock of hair from her hot face. She was just not good at selling herself. Which was odd for someone who worked in the marketing business. But maybe once she got the job, she'd feel more validated and entitled to stand up for herself. Then it would have been proven beyond a doubt that she was good at what she did.

Outside a car horn honked. Lily put her phone away and walked out onto the porch. A big old Mercedes stood in the yard and a man with a cowboy hat stepped out, waving a hand at her. "Hello, you must be Lily Roberts, the marketing lady? Mrs. Jenkins told me all about you. I'm Bud Travers. I'm here to offer my services for the Apple Fest." He shoved back his cowboy hat and gave her a winning smile. "I used to be part of it when the Cloverdales were still organizing. I was really sorry when it ended. We always had such good fun. You wanting to bring it back to life, well, it's like you read my mind. I've been waiting for such a fairy godmother to stop by for years." He reached into the back of his car and produced a cowboy hat much like the one he was wearing. "This is for you. You have to look the part in this district. Try it on. Should fit but if anything is wrong with it, or you don't like the color, I can change it. I sell hats like this, belts, boots… It's my bread and butter."

Lily accepted the hat and put it on her head. "It fits like it was made for me."

"I have an eye for it. I saw you in town yesterday and thought that little lady needs to look more ranch girl. You're from the city, right? Nothing wrong with that. We need a new wind here. To shake things up. I just hadn't expected it to be blowing from the Williams ranch. Cade is more uh…traditional you know. Like his father was. I was really close with his old man." Bud nodded solemnly. "Now, I'd like to know how many participants you'd want in the prettiest pig contest."

"Excuse me?" Lily asked.

"We always have a beauty contest at Apple Fest. Not for pretty girls but for sows. Every farmer who has a few delivers his best sow for the competition. And we choose a winner. I say we, but of course you need to select a jury."

"Could you be on it?"

"I'd be honored, but I'm entering my own sow. Now, that would make me prejudiced wouldn't it? It would have to be someone who doesn't enter. Maybe um… Cade and yourself? You'd make a handsome couple presiding over the piggy pageant."

Lily cringed for a moment wondering what her colleagues would think if they ever learned she had been on the jury to select the best sow of the county, but then if it had always been a part of Apple Fest, the tradition should be honored. "I'll add it to the list then."

"Great, thank you." He took off his hat as he made a deep bow. "Much obliged. Now I have to run because I have customers waiting for me at the shop. See you later."

Lily shook her head with a grin as the whirlwind visitor stepped into his old Mercedes again and started the engine. The car bucked as it began to move. In a cloud of exhaust fumes it departed down the driveway.

Lily felt the hat on her head. How did it look on her? She went into the house and stood in front of the hall mirror turning left and right. She did look more like a cowgirl now she supposed.

"Hey, where did you get that?" a voice asked behind her back.

Lily flushed and turned away from the mirror. Ever since the moments in the barn she felt a little uncomfortable around Cade. He had been so tender brushing her tears away and holding her and it had felt like there was a real connection between them.

"I kind of like it," she said, taking the hat off and turning it around in her hands. "It's a gift from Bud Travers. He was just here to talk about the pig pageant."

"Oh no." Cade rushed over to her and grabbed her arm. "Tell me you told him we're not doing that. Ever. Again."

The honest concern in his eyes punched her gut and her heart missed a beat. "Uh… Is something wrong with that?"

"The pig pageant always created chaos. Cows you can groom and lead in front of a jury, but pigs? No way. They have a mind of their own. They break loose, break down stalls, destroy pies that were supposed to be judged later. It's a disaster and we should *never ever* have a pig pageant again."

Lily cringed. "I uh…didn't know and told him it was okay."

"I should have warned you. But don't you worry, it can be set right." Cade reached into his pocket. "I've got to call him right away and…" He stared at the screen. "Oh no."

"What?"

"He already shared the news in a few message groups. It will be bigger and better than ever before. The jury will be…" Cade's mouth fell open.

Lily shuffled her feet and said nothing.

"'Lily Roberts and Cade Williams,'" Cade read slowly. "For real? Or is he just making this up as he goes?"

"I might have said that it was okay if… I had no idea…"

"My father sat in that jury when I was ten. He awarded the ribbon to one man's pig and then had discussions with three others for the rest of the year because they thought their sow had been better and they even accused him of having accepted bribes to award the ribbon the way he did. My father said never again. He kept recalling the disaster every next Apple Fest and told me to stay away from judging for the rest of my life. Now you…"

"Bud Travers said your father and he were best of friends."

Cade sighed. "I admit he's a smooth talker and he did bring you a gift…"

Lily felt terrible. Her cheeks were on fire and the hat weighed a ton in her hands. Almost like that alleged bribe Cade had just mentioned. "I could give it back and explain…"

"Nah. He has already made the announcement and I don't want to put you in a spot. We have to go through with it now. But next time before you decide on an addition to the program you discuss it with me."

"Yes, sir." It really seemed like the moments in the barn together had mellowed him. Earlier he had been so touchy about her deciding on things without consulting him. But now there was an understanding of sorts. She should be glad for it, and she was, but it was also confusing. A warning sign flashed in the back of her mind that if Cade started being so nice she might actually grow to like him. And this was just a cooperation, a business thing.

Cade pulled the hat from her hands and put it on her head. He stepped back and gave her a critical once-over. "Hmm, more like this." He pulled the brim of the hat down a fraction. "Better. A real country girl." He leaned over. "How much do you know about pigs? If you're going to be on a jury, you better have an idea what you're going to judge."

Lily stared into his sparkling blue eyes. She didn't know what to say. She knew nothing about pigs. "You can teach me all I need to know, right? I don't want to look like a fool."

"We should spend some time going over the essentials. Looking at pictures of prize pigs and…maybe see some for real? Have you got some time tonight? We could do a pig tour and then…eat ice cream?"

Lily held his gaze. A small voice inside told her this wasn't a good idea. She had too much to do and…spending time with Cade was fine as long as they were working on the project. But free time together? Moments where it might get personal and…

Nonsense. He was inviting her on a tour of…sows for a pig pageant. It wasn't personal. It was work. And that was just the way it should be.

"I THINK I'M still going to be dreaming about pigs tonight," Lily said when they drove away from the second ranch they'd visited. Cade had pointed out a few things to look for: how the pigs stood on their legs, if they were perky, had nice ears and a good curly tail, etcetera, but mainly it came down to a personal judgment about the appearance of the pig. "It's also a chance for the community to showcase what the ranchers are proud of and have a bit of appreciation for it."

"Participating is more important than winning, huh?" she had said with a grin. "Just like in the Olympics."

"Yeah, and just like in the Olympics everyone wants to win the gold medal anyway."

Cade smiled to himself. He felt relaxed. He let the wheel run through his fingers as they headed for the ice cream parlor in the next town. He had told Lily that it was closer than going back to Heartmont, which wasn't one hundred percent true but as she didn't know the area well, she wouldn't be aware of that. He knew what would happen the instant he turned up at the ice cream window in Heartmont with a woman by his side. Mrs. Peters would grab her phone and call all her friends to speculate about what Cade Williams was up to. He would rather not be the talk of the town.

Not yet anyway. He bet that the jungle drum would start beating anyway once they were seen together at the Apple Fest. He'd make sure to tell everyone Lily was the marketing expert who had put the festival together to imprint on the minds of people it was a business thing. But he knew how they'd nod and think, yeah, sure, Williams, but we can see she's pretty so what are you hiding from us?

It was just that he didn't like people deciding for him what he was feeling. Especially as he wasn't sure himself.

Cade glanced at Lily. "Have you thought about what flavors you're going to have? Don't expect them to carry anything fancy like big-city ice cream parlors do. They have got strawberry and cherry and a few more and that's it. But you can get whipped cream on top and sprinkles."

"Fine with me." Lily turned her head and eyed him earnestly. "Are you thinking this parlor is out of my league?"

Cade cringed that she recalled his words

and harked back to them. "I'm just… Well, this is the place I've known for all of my life and I like it, but I have no idea how someone sees it who comes in from the outside. I don't want you to have the wrong expectations of it. This morning you mentioned in passing that your boss is in Paris at the moment for a client. In a few years' time that could be you jetting around the world. You organized Gina's wedding where my little sister was dressed in… What was the designer's name?"

"Carolina Herrera."

"Yes, well, all I remember is that Gina let slip what it had cost and it was more than two cows."

"A wedding is a special occasion. You go big or you go home."

"Really?" He had never thought of it that way. "It's just one day in your life."

"It's the most romantic day of your life. Hopefully, also meaningful and loving. Where memories are made to last forever. My mother had been dreaming of a family wedding for years. Every now and then she'd mention what venue she envisioned, what kind of cake and what kind of dress.

It was of course meant to prime me for my big day. But Barry met Gina and…from there it was about their dream wedding for my mother. She told me incessantly how it had to be." She gave him an apologetic smile. "I just wanted it to be the day my mom had dreamed of for so long. And Gina loved the fairy-tale quality of it. I did discuss it with her. It's not like we decided it all over her head. I just wanted everyone to have a great day. I guess Barry would have been happy if it had been barefoot on the beach… He was impulsive and… My mom worried he'd drag Gina to Vegas and do it there, just for the kick of it, you know. She wanted to keep some sort of…rein on the situation."

Aha. "So your brother has always been like that. Doing things on a whim…"

"He didn't commit to Gina on a whim. He loved her." Lily looked at him with an earnest conviction in her eyes. "But Barry wasn't about formalities. He wanted to express that love for her in a special way. That's why he had all of these ideas. Like they could get married in a hot air balloon over the desert or something." She smiled. "It would have been super romantic."

"And impractical. How do you get an entire wedding party into a hot air balloon?"

"Just the two of them and the official who had to ask the questions." Lily grinned.

Cade was stunned at the idea. "And what about your family then?" he queried. "Parents, you?"

"I think it's a personal moment for the two people involved. If they want to keep it to themselves, they can."

"I guess so." Cade hadn't really considered it in that light before. Country weddings involved the entire community. He was used to that and had never questioned the practice. "But your mother was worried he'd run off and do it like that?"

"Yes. And that wasn't what she wanted. She was very upset at the idea. So I stepped up and offered to organize and make everyone happy." She shrugged. "I guess I felt sort of responsible for how it turned out. Maybe it was a bit much. But a wedding day is a sort of fairy tale. It need not resemble real life. The bride can be a princess and have a really special castle-like venue for the day. It's something you should re-member just because it's so extraordinary."

"I suppose." Cade gestured with a hand. "We're used to country weddings here. Do the vows outside, grab a few snacks, dance all night long. It's not big and fancy at all but sort of…homegrown. Rooted in the community."

LILY WAS ABOUT to blurt out she was happy she didn't live here, but swallowed it down as it was rude. Still it felt like he almost meant: I step away from work for an hour, say I do in my overalls, toast with a few friends and then back to normal as soon as possible. Where was the special feeling in that? The romance?

It did seem like romance didn't exist in Cade's book. He was so down-to-earth and practical, he would probably wonder why bother with romance at all? When he had still had this girlfriend, Shelby, had they ever been on outings, dates? Had he sur-prised her with gifts or…

Not everybody shows love in the same way, she reminded herself. *Your parents raised you with gifts and stuff and Barry*

*took that into his life too much. He used
money as a way to show affection. But
other people are different. They show it
by...being there or listening or...*

Fine, she retorted to herself, *but a wedding day needs frills. Period.*

"Here we are." Cade parked the car and
came round to let her get out. The ice cream
parlor had a cute bench in front where they
could sit. Cade pointed out the list with flavors. "It's gotten longer since the last time
I've been here," he observed.

"It sure has. I see tiramisu and mango.
But I'd love some triple chocolate and apple
honey. A local specialty is just what I want
to try."

Cade ordered while Lily sat down on
the bench. They were a little away from
the main street and a bird sang overhead.
It was quiet and she stretched her legs
suddenly feeling she was tired. She had
answered emails about Apple Fest and dis-
cussed more details for the day's schedule
and what time people could start setting up
their booths. She had also engaged some
musicians because despite the fun idea of
her and Wayne performing she did think

they needed a really good group to accompany the dancing. There'd be a BBQ and fireworks at the end.

"Here." Cade leaned over to hand her the ice cream cone. Their fingers touched as she accepted it, carefully balancing the cone with its huge scoops. Cade had also asked for whipped cream on top. "You can use this." He gave her a small wooden spoon. "And napkins of course."

She spread them across her lap and then enjoyed the first bites of ice cream. The apple honey was deliciously fresh and the triple chocolate balanced it with a creamy sweetness. She closed her eyes a moment. "This is perfect."

Cade ate his ice cream in silence. She studied his tight profile. "What kind of wedding would you like? I mean, you seem to know exactly what you don't want, but you must have some idea of what you do want."

"In the past it was all very clear to me. Later on… I'm thirty-two now, you know." He gestured with his free hand. "Everyone I know around here is married. The guys I used to hang out with have kids."

"Wayne is still single."

"Yeah, but he doesn't want a relationship."

"Oh, and you do?"

"Let's put it like this. I would have wanted to be married by now with a family. Just being settled, having all your ducks in a row."

"The way it should be?"

"I guess so." He gave her an ironic grimace. "Guess we both value perfect pictures after all?"

Lily shrugged. "I do understand what you mean. People always assume I'm in a relationship or at least looking for one. But I never bumped into a handsome man in the subway and internet dating feels so superficial. I guess I really need to know someone before I can get to appreciate them and feelings develop from there."

"You don't believe in instant attraction?"

She took her time scooping ice cream into her mouth before replying, "What good is it if you're poles apart? You have to make the relationship work and how could you without common ground?"

"Right. Ma had a hard time settling here on the ranch. She wasn't a country girl, you know. Met my dad at a convention in Aurora. She worked the reception at the hotel where he was staying. It was love at first sight for them." Cade's features softened in a smile. "She was willing to give up her job and all her connections to move here. She thought she wasn't moving to the other end of the country. But it might as well have been. Her own words." He looked at her. "She couldn't have a quick cup of coffee with a friend on her lunch break. Heartmont doesn't have a cinema or a theater. She had to learn a lot about the ranch. It was hard. I can understand why women don't want to date ranchers. And those who do, often have an overly romantic idea about ranch life."

He smiled sadly. "Maybe that's why the idea of selling our lifestyle to city people rubs me the wrong way. Because it's always different when you've truly been there and lived that life and experienced how much it costs and not everyone can cope with it. I guess that behind every idyllic photograph I see the sweat and tears of farmers trying to survive. Young people move away from the area, there are few takers for ranches which might have been family owned for six generations. That's hard to stomach. The entire landscape of my childhood is changing. I guess I uh… feel responsible to help ranchers in trouble and keep businesses alive. Maybe I'm too fanatic about it." He rubbed his neck with a weary look. "I'm sorry that you have to deal with my frustration. It has nothing to do with you."

"I guess we could both try not to let outside influences ruin our relationship. Working relationship. I mean, we do have things in common. We love animals. And ice cream."

Now Cade had to laugh. "That's a start." Her phone beeped and she let him hold her ice cream while she checked it. "Work." She glanced over a few emails. "I have to reply to these. Do you mind…"

"Nope, fine with me."

CADE STUDIED LILY as she was reading some attachment at top speed, then adding a few comments. She was fully focused on the task at hand. She knew what she was doing, moreover, she loved what she was doing. And he really wanted her to have that chance to get her dream job. What she had told him so far built an image of someone who had often dismissed her own wants and needs, made them second to someone else's. She had felt obliged to step up and organize the wedding, to come back to the pizzeria when Gina had been pregnant with the twins. Now it was her season. This project, the revival of Apple Fest, could get her settled into a new life after the old had been swept away. He wanted her to succeed. And he needed to do everything in his power to make the new Apple Fest the best it could be.

"There." Lily lowered the phone. "Oh quickly..." She took the cone from his hand and ensured the melting ice cream ended up in her mouth and not on her clothes. "The girls would love this. Maybe we can bring them someday and let Gina have a bit of time to herself."

"Time to herself?" he asked, not understanding.

"Yes, to do something without a little girl or two clinging to her arms. She can't always care for others. She also has to care for herself." Lily frowned. "Maybe I can get her booked with a beautician for a treatment? Just a facial and a manicure."

Cade almost choked on his ice cream. "Excuse me? Where do you think you can rustle up a beautician around these parts?"

Lily ignored the questions and enthused, "In Saint Paul we used to go to manicures together lots of times. It's fun. You get a nice drink, they do your nails while you sit back and relax and chat."

Cade looked at Lily's nails. They didn't have glittery stones or anything on them. Not even nail polish. "I would never have guessed. Does it go with your rock climbing?"

"I haven't had time for that in a while." She shrugged.

"Sounds to me like you're the one who needs the me time."

"I can't now. I have the project and Gina and the kids to look after. It's really important to me to get this right. You asked earlier about my mom and dad. If they ever come to see me in Denver. No, they don't. They don't think I should be there. I should come and live with them at the resort. Help them out with marketing, do their social media. But I can't do it. I don't want to be taken in because I am the boss's daughter. I need to prove what I can do. On my own. You understand?"

"I do. I made changes to the ranch, cutting back on cattle and making it more about the orchards and the flowers to put my stamp on it. I felt like I needed to… contribute to it in a bigger way than just be the next Williams to take over. Dad's death threw me into the deep, much sooner than I had ever expected, and… It had to somehow become more my ranch. Because if you're going to put so much time and energy into something, it better be worth it, right?"

She held up her phone to him. "This is worth it. This chance to become one of the team. It's not about whether I ever get to Dubai. But about showing them what I am made of."

He nodded. It was weird how this infuriating city girl who liked manicures and big weddings said things he could totally relate to. How she made him see that it was a good idea to break away and have ice cream and not be the rancher but…

Yeah, what anyway? What was he when it wasn't the rancher, the regional representative, the dutiful son, the big brother who took care of everything? Who was Cade Williams on his own?

He shifted weight uncomfortably. "Look, we should really be getting back. Ma said the washing machine made a funny noise this morning so maybe I should have a look at it before it breaks down on the next wash. With those little girls around we have a lot more laundry."

"Yeah." Lily finished her cone. "Thanks for this. It was fun."

"Don't mention it." He got up and headed for the SUV. He had a sneaky feeling he was somehow running. But he didn't know exactly from what or why.

CHAPTER TEN

"THANKS, MRS. MULLINS. I look forward to seeing you then." Lily disconnected and looked at Mrs. Williams who was repairing a hole in a sock. The past few days had been a blur of calls and emails to ensure booths were the right size, there was a varied offer of crafts and food and so on. It gave her energy to see the event take shape, but it was also a lot of responsibility to make sure everything was taken care of and there wouldn't be any last-minute problems. "Mrs. Mullins will be at the Apple Fest baking her apple fritters."

"Oh, that's great. She always made the most delicious creations. I think she even won a prize with them at a state-wide competition for best fritters. You have to ask her about her trophy. She's so proud of it."

Lily made a mental note to do just that. She wrote Mrs. Mullins's name in a booth on the schedule in front of her. "I just have one more booth to fill. That went fast."

"People want to be part of a community thing. Now more than ever. The storm hit us hard and...well, we need a bit of togetherness. And as you're doing all the organizing for us, it doesn't take too much time away from the necessary repairs." Mrs. Williams smiled at her. "Thanks for making this possible for us."

Lily looked back down at the paper to make the *M* of *Mullins* more readable. She always felt uncomfortable receiving compliments. A little voice in the back of her head kept saying that people liked what she did now, but that it could change if she made a mistake. That she needed to prove herself worthy of this recognition.

Her phone rang and she looked at the screen. Wayne. She accepted the call. "What's up, cowboy?"

From the corner of her eye she saw Gina come into the kitchen. She went to the sink to get herself a glass of water. Rosie walked over to Gina for a scratch behind the ears, but she turned her head in the direction of the phone as soon as Wayne began to play for Lily. He had created another silly song he wanted her to hear. As he plunked away at his guitar singing about apples that weren't coming off the trees, Lily laughed till her cheeks hurt. He was really something.

"I'm not going to sing that with you. I couldn't. I'd be falling apart halfway through in a fit of the giggles."

"I'm just trying to write an appropriate song." Wayne feigned hurt. "You told me it had to be something special. Not just a rendition of 'Achy Breaky Heart.'"

"Keep trying," Lily said with a grin.

CADE LAY ON his knees in front of the washing machine and watched as the excess water from a little hatch in front flowed into a bowl he had placed underneath it. It was supposed to help when the machine was acting up. He could of course also remove the back panel and have a look at the entire wire spaghetti inside but he'd rather not if he could avoid it.

"Hey." Gina stuck her head around the door. "How is it coming along?"

"Great. Will be fixed in no time."

"Good. Say, that performance of Wayne and Lily is going to be entertainment gold. They are so much fun together." Gina leaned against the doorjamb, with a smile on her face. "I was thinking. If they fell in love, Lily could stay around Heartmont. I mean she could come around more often and in the long run she might even come to live here permanently."

"With Wayne?" Cade asked. He sat up and eyed Gina with tilted head. "Are you serious? That man's household is a mess. You don't really want to land your friend in such a pigsty, do you?"

"Lily can clean it up and teach him to do chores." Gina winked at him. "When a man is in love, he suddenly knows how to vacuum and do the dishes. I think Wayne is trying so hard for this performance because he is a little in love with Lily."

Cade rubbed his neck. "Wayne's just eager for the spotlight. Why do you always assume feelings are behind a man's actions?"

Gina straightened up and flashed her eyes at him. "Give me one good reason why he wouldn't be in love with Lily? She's pretty, has heart. She loves animals so it would be perfect for his horses and his dog breeding."

He couldn't deny any of those things. But how pretty she was or how good with animals wasn't really the point. "Lily is a city girl. She wants to live in Denver and have this high-flying job. She's not going to bury herself in the countryside." *She has something to prove, to herself and her parents.* He wasn't going to say that. She had told him in a personal moment and he wasn't sure Gina knew or that Lily even wanted her to know. They all had to protect Gina and the unborn baby from any form of stress.

"Hmmm. If the feeling is right… Wayne makes her laugh. I love to see her laugh and be happy. She's so serious working for our Apple Fest all the time. I hope we're not asking too much of her."

See, there you had it. Gina immediately worried about others, felt responsible for them. "Of course not. Lily loves her work. I mean, she's always answering some email or taking calls. I told her not to work too hard, but she just gave me a dirty look and continued anyway. I think she is a worka-holic at heart."

"From one who knows." Gina grimaced. "Honestly, don't you think she and Wayne could make a good couple? The girls would also love to have her closer to us. It's Auntie Lily this, and Auntie Lily that, all day long. Imagine her living just a few minutes away from us. She could pop over every day."

Somehow Cade didn't think it was a good idea, but he didn't want to analyze exactly why. The washing machine had stopped giving water and he carefully cleaned the pipe before shutting the hatch. "That should do it."

"Thanks, Cade, you're great with those things. Look… Next time you talk to Wade, couldn't you uh…sing Lily's praises to him and see how he responds? You're best friends, you should be able to get some-thing out of him. If I ask, he won't tell me anything. But you could go there, have a beer and a heart-to-heart."

"That's not how male friendships work," Cade protested. He didn't want to think of the moment where Wade would tell him that he was in love with Lily. His gut feeling said it would be a disaster and even if he didn't want to investigate why, he trusted his gut feeling.

Gina said, "Come on, you could do your sis a favor. I want to keep Lily around. Once she's settled in Denver and buried in work, she won't come back here."

Like you never came back here once you were married to Barry, Cade thought. But he didn't say it. He didn't want to talk to Gina about Barry because he knew she'd start crying and he couldn't handle that. He didn't want to be the one to make her sad. She had to find healing here, and recover so she could be there for her children. The girls and the baby that was growing inside of her. Cade had to protect her against pain, not inflict it by asking hard questions. The past was the past. It was over, didn't matter anymore.

"I'll see what I can do," he heard himself say.

"I knew you'd come round." Gina darted over to him, hugged him and kissed him on the cheek. "Thanks, big brother. I can always rely on you."

"Sure," Cade grunted. After she had left,

he stood there a moment staring at the washing machine. Wayne had revived the Heartmont Heroes. He had used it as a clever way to engage Lily and be in touch with her daily. Was he flirting with her? Or was he just clowning around as Wayne often did?

If it was just a joke to him, Lily might get the wrong impression and feel hurt. That would drive her away from Heartmont and frustrate Gina's purpose of seeing more of her sister-in-law and having her around for the girls' sake. So to help Gina and the twins, Cade had to ensure that Wayne didn't hurt Lily. Now how could he possibly do that when the two of them were constantly talking about their upcoming performance and getting together to practice and…

By being a part of it too?

Cade perked up. That was it. What a brilliant solution, even if he said so himself.

He hurriedly went to his bedroom and opened the big closet against the wall. There deep inside the closet's darkest depths, hidden against the back wall, in a cloth cover, was his guitar. He hadn't touched it in years. Not since he had sat down to write the song for Gina's wedding.

Cade halted with his hand on the cloth cover, reluctant to pull out the guitar and be reminded of the hopes with which he had created his song. He had wanted to show Gina how much he loved her. He had wanted her to feel the connection with home even though she got married and moved away. But Barry hadn't been waiting for a tug on the heartstrings about the life she left behind.

Now that he had talked to Lily about the fairy-tale character that weddings were supposed to have, he did understand her actions better. And maybe it was time to look hard at his old grudge and realize it hadn't been about his song as much as it had been about the reality of letting his little sister go. Losing her to another man who would be most important to her. Maybe he had resented Barry's generosity because he had seen how Gina enjoyed being pampered and it had confronted him with the fact that they hadn't been able to provide her with that at home. It had felt like failure, while it wasn't a competition of course. He should have been happy that Barry was so thoughtful and gave her all those things.

It was high time he let go of that bitterness inside. The past was over and today was a new day.

With determination he fetched the guitar. It was time to start making music again. With his pal Wayne, with Lily. The Heartmont Heroes were back in town.

Cade grinned as he carried his guitar into the kitchen. Lily sat at the table, one leg pulled up under her. Her long blond hair hung loose over her shoulders as she leaned over a large sheet of paper, working something out on a separate sheet. He stood and looked at her a moment, how the light of the lamp played across her smooth features and the concentration made her pucker her lips a touch. It was nice to have her here. He could understand Gina's wish to keep her around.

But not as Wayne's girlfriend.

She looked up and said, "Hi. What's that?"

He glanced down at the guitar in his hand. "I uh… I thought I'd pop over to Wayne's for a bit to see how we sound together."

LILY STARED AT the guitar in Cade's hand. She had known he had played it in the band and had even seen old photos, but still this moment was a bit surreal. Somehow she couldn't really envision practical down-to-earth Cade as the sensitive type who played the guitar. But maybe it had nothing to do with being sensitive. Maybe he liked to play country music and unwind after a hard day's work?

"I can't come along," she said. "I have to work out more details for the fair and I also have a few things to read for work."

"Oh, I didn't count on you coming at all. It's just a guys' thing."

Great, thanks for telling me after *I almost invited myself.* Lily tried to keep smiling. "Have fun."

He left the room with Rosie in tow and soon after she heard the engine of his SUV start. Gina came into the kitchen carrying a houseplant. "Poor thing didn't get enough water. I'm going to soak him under the tap for a bit to see if he perks up. Is Cade off again?"

"Yes, he wanted to see Wayne."

"Oh." Gina's expression changed as if

she was secretly amused about something. Or satisfied?

Lily frowned, a suspicious feeling settling in her chest. "Are those two up to something? Do you know more about what that might be?"

Gina flushed and turned away, fussing with the plant. "No, not really."

That is a yes, Lily thought. Her friend was such a bad liar. Had Wayne persuaded Cade to be part of the band again for a reason? She just hoped that with the two of them together they wouldn't come up with even sillier antics. She did want to keep the performance classy. Solid. In tune with the rest of the program.

But maybe she was out of line there? The Apple Fest belonged to this community. They were entitled to their traditions and their kind of entertainment. Was she butting in too much because she was concerned about how it would look in the media coverage? She did have a very personal stake in all of this. Was the pressure to succeed getting the better of her?

It had happened before. Cade's questions about Gina's wedding day had painfully reminded her. The gorgeous princess dress, the tiara, the top venue and the live band… Gina and Barry had loved it, Mom and Dad had loved it. She had fulfilled all of their wishes, but by organizing the wedding as she had, she had created the first debts that Barry had ever owed. She had believed he could cover all the expenses, but he had told her later that he had had to borrow money. Had he felt forced into it? Had he not been able to say no to the more expensive elements of the day? Because of Mom and his bride-to-be and… Had Barry suffered from the same pressure to live up to expectations as she had?

She wished she had asked him. That she knew why he hadn't talked about the money issue. But he was gone and she could only speculate. Also about her own part in what had unfolded. It had been so normal in their family to have money for everything. You could simply not say that you couldn't afford it or at least had to save for it. Had Barry felt like a failure for not being able to run the restaurant like Mom and Dad had? It had gone downhill after he took over.

Lily rubbed her eyes. She didn't want to think about it, but the thoughts forced themselves into her head. Barry didn't have Dad's magical touch with the staff. He was too lenient because he wanted to be liked and then suddenly when he felt his authority was slipping, he got angry and alienated people with his rude remarks. Then she had caught him slipping bills into a drawer unopened.

Lily leaned back in her chair. She should have urged him to get help. A financial coach or debt counseling or something. She shouldn't have let it go on. But she had wanted him to solve his own problems, if only so he discovered that he could. She had believed that he should take responsibility and that it would build his confidence. But it had only allowed things to get offtrack even more. Until the situation had been irreparable.

Her phone beeped and she checked the emails. Her colleague Cynthia asked a brief question about a new data analysis program. She decided to call her to explain in person. Cynthia followed her instructions and sighed with relief. "Thanks, Lily.

You're so good with the computer stuff. When you explain it, it's simple. But when left to my own devices… Say, how are you doing out there?"

"It's nice and quiet here. I can get loads of work done." Lily felt obliged to add the latter so it wouldn't look like a vacation at the firm's expense.

"Yeah, and it has nothing to do with that hot guy?"

"What hot guy?" Lily queried.

"The cowboy. He walked across the screen during our last conference call."

Lily flushed. "Oh. That's my brother-in-law."

"Oh. I didn't know you have a sister?"

"No, my brother was married to his sister."

"Aren't they together anymore?"

Lily took a deep breath before replying, "My brother died this spring."

"Oh, I'm sorry. How terrible. He must have been pretty young. Was it an accident?"

"Yes, he was out skiing with friends and they got caught in an avalanche. The others were unharmed, but they couldn't find him under the snow and he died before they could get help."

"I see. That sounds awful."

"His wife was pregnant so she moved back with her mother here on the ranch to have help with their other two children. Twin girls." Lily swallowed past the lump in her throat. "I'm helping out where I can and organizing fundraising since the ranch got hit by a storm."

"Feels like all the bad luck in the world piled up on these people. Is there a website where I can make a donation?"

"Yes, there is a page for the community, to raise funds to help those with the most damage. I can send you the link."

"Great. Sorry about the hot guy comment. I thought you were settled in the countryside on some ranch-style B and B thing. But with all that going on, romance must be the last thing on your mind. Do send me the link and I'll make a donation for those folks. Thanks for helping me with the computer stuff. Talk to you later."

Lily sat staring at the screen of her phone long after it had gone black. It was rather odd to know that an outsider saw Cade as a hot guy. But he was good-looking, she guessed, and strong and dependable. No arguing about that. Their work for Apple Fest had also created a better relationship between them, even a level of understanding. She had started organizing this big event thinking it was too bad she had to do it with Cade, and now she was…enjoying it? Sort of.

That was the whole point, right? Doing something because you loved it and enjoyed it and your heart was in it. She had to have faith that if she gave her best for Apple Fest, it would also give back to her.

CHAPTER ELEVEN

THE BIG DAY had finally arrived and Cade walked across the meadow allotted for the Apple Fest. It was 5:30 and the man who delivered the booths to them backed his truck into the field. A Jeep that had followed it parked and released four able-looking young men who were going to put the booths together.

The morning air was fresh and crisp and the weather forecast had announced a beautiful summer day. Soon this empty green field would be turned into a fairground buzzing with people. The idea made Cade's blood tingle. He had worked hard for this day and he was now eager to see results.

But it was more than that. He also wanted to see Lily again. She had left a week ago for Denver to check on her apartment, meet her colleagues, do in-person work stuff and in general keep her life on track since she'd been away for a while. After she had lived with them for three weeks, the ranch hadn't seemed the same without her. It had been quiet and Gina had observed several times how great it would be if Lily and Wayne got together so her friend would stay around town. She had quizzed Cade about his proposed heart-to-heart with Wayne and Cade had said he was certain that Wayne was just his usual sociable self around Lily. That it might look like more, but it certainly wasn't. Gina's obvious disappointment had made Cade itch under the collar. How could she seriously consider Lily dating a commitment-phobe like Wayne just to keep her here? It was a disastrous idea.

He directed a booth in place and showed the young men how the rest should be laid out. "We want to keep a large enough space free to corral off for the pig pageant."

"The what?"

"Election of the most beautiful pig. Courtesy of Bud Travers." Cade resisted the urge to roll his eyes. Lily should never have agreed to it. But she had. And he couldn't really blame her.

He had missed her while she was away

and now he really just wanted to see her and do things together with her, show her the apples that had been harvested and the two calves that had been born.

But she had arrived on the ranch late last night when he had been out with a friend helping with a difficult birth of a foal. And he couldn't possibly have woken her at 5:00 a.m. to see to this booth-building thing.

He stretched and yawned. The crisp air seemed to slither under his sleeves and made goose bumps crawl across his back. He also wished he had brought a thermos of coffee.

"Good morning!"

He swirled round to the cheerful voice. Lily came bouncing up to him in a red dress and cowboy boots. She wore the hat Travers had gifted her. In her right hand she clutched her phone, in the left…a thermos?

"I thought you could use a cup of strong coffee. It's going to be a long day. But the weather looks good." She peered up at the sky a moment. "No rain or hard wind. I'm so excited for today. You?"

He had almost forgotten how deep brown her eyes were and how long her lashes. How wide her smile and how infectious the good vibes in her voice as she spoke. He suddenly felt warm all over as if she had wrapped him in a hug.

"You should have stayed in bed a little longer," he said. "You had the drive out here, last night."

"I couldn't possibly sleep anymore. It feels like my birthday." She grinned at him. "Rosie felt the same way. She wanted to come with me, but I told her later. With the booths being built and all, I'd worry she'd be run underfoot."

"That's right. I bet she pulled her pleading face though."

"She sure did. But I didn't cave. Here, have the coffee." She put her phone in an impossibly small red cross-body purse and opened the thermos. "I had some on the ranch."

The splatter of the coffee made his heart sing. And that delicious scent... She knew how to treat a man.

"How have things been while I was away?" she asked.

"Quiet."

"Quiet? I thought there was still so much to do before the big day."

"Yes, of course lots of loose ends to tie up. I meant uh…" *It was quiet without you?* That would sound odd. But he had missed her enthusiasm over small victories, the care she put into setting the table, all the little things that brought a certain lightness to his life that was otherwise missing. He nursed his coffee. "But it's all worked out. You can rest assured that things will go down without a hitch today."

"I never doubted that. I know you're Mr. Organization. Wayne told me what you've done over the years, for the community."

Wayne, huh. "Did you talk to him much while you were in Denver?"

"Every day. He video called me to show off the puppies. They are so cute and they grow up so fast."

Hmmm. It suddenly occurred to him that he could also have video called her to show the newborn calves.

"And we had to practice of course. I also asked if you shouldn't be part of the call, but he said it wasn't necessary as he practiced separately with you."

"Exactly." Cade forced a smile. "It'll be fine. We're on when the BBQ is about to start. People will be more interested in getting a burger and salad than paying much attention to us."

"Good. Then I need not have stage fright." Lily looked up at him with questioning eyes as if she wanted him to reassure her. But her intense gaze made him sort of uncomfortable and a bit at a loss for words. He should tell her he had missed her, but the best moment for that had passed. He should have done it right away when she asked how things had been. *It was quiet without you. I missed you.* How hard would it have been to say that?

"More coffee," he mumbled and focused on the thermos.

YOU COULD SAY you like my dress, Lily thought.

Then again maybe he didn't like it? Or he hadn't even noticed it was new. She had often heard from friends and colleagues that men never saw new clothes or even new haircuts so maybe it was a universal thing. Nothing special to Cade. Not reflecting on their relationship, on her or whatever.

She almost shook her head. This was the big day and getting everything just right was her top priority. She had worked so hard for this and she intended to reap the rewards. Tonight she'd have a big event to her name, the perfect material to wow her boss and even convince skeptical Eva Bailey that she could do the job.

She looked at the men putting up the booths. "They do it so fast."

"Yep, but then they do this every day. In a different place, wherever they are wanted. I agreed with the booth owners to arrive around eight o'clock to dress up their booths. I know some of them will be early so I made sure this will all be standing well ahead of their arrival. The hay bales should also be coming in any minute now."

"Hay bales?" She couldn't recall having asked for those.

"Yes, partly for dressing up the scene and partly for creating some barriers around areas, etcetera. It's practical but also gives a rural touch. You'll see." He sipped his coffee. His blue shirt echoed the color of his eyes and his hair was still wet from the shower. If Cynthia were here, she would probably start again about how good-looking he was. Lily was glad she wasn't coming over to fawn over him.

"Did you have a chance last night to talk to Gina and see the girls?" Cade asked.

"The girls were already in bed, but I did peek in to watch them sleeping. They're so cute. I can't wait to snap photos of them at the fair today." Lily checked her watch. "Your mother is coming over here around eight thirty with the animals."

They had agreed to bring Mollie, Millie and some smaller animals to create a little petting zoo. Mrs. Williams and Gina would supervise it and ensure the animals weren't overwhelmed if there was a lot of interest in them.

Cade nodded.

A car horn honked and a dark blue station wagon breezed onto the terrain. It stopped beside the Jeep of the booth builders and a woman stepped out. She had gray hair tied back in a ponytail and wore a paisley blouse with jeans. She dove into the back of the station wagon and pulled out a large twined basket. "Good morning!" She waved at them.

Cade hitched a brow. "It's the mayor's wife," he said. "What is she doing here at this hour? Her husband's opening speech is scheduled for 9:30, right?"

"Right."

The woman walked over, navigating the patchy grass with the huge basket in her arms. She also clutched a leash with an adorable beagle puppy pulling in all directions.

"Go and help her," Lily urged Cade.

He handed her the thermos and went over, accepting the basket. "Oh thanks," the mayor's wife said. "It's heavy. I thought…" She leaned down to pick up the puppy. "That you'd want some breakfast being so busy at this early hour. Hello." She smiled at Lily. "We haven't formally met. Dakota Riley. My husband is mayor of Heartmont. We so appreciate you choosing our town to promote and get more tourists to the area. My husband will give a little speech later today and he'll be expressing his thanks then too, but I felt I had to do something more…practical." She patted the basket which Cade was still holding. "Do we have a table here?"

"Not yet, but we can use one of the booths," Cade said. He carried the basket over. Mrs. Riley followed.

"What an adorable puppy," Lily enthused.

"Yes, but he's a handful. Has to be watched constantly, or he's doing something naughty like chewing up my husband's best shoes. My husband had made me swear I wouldn't get a new dog after our beloved Belle died this spring, but the house felt so empty. I visited someone who showed me a litter of these cute beagles and this little fellow came straight at me. It felt like he chose me to come and live with. Didn't you, little rascal?" She cuddled the dog in her arms. "At night I'm bushed, but hey…the things we do for love."

At the booth Cade opened the basket and started to unpack sandwiches, bottles of apple juice and donuts. The men gathered round with appreciative grunts and comments. They started eating. Mrs. Riley said to Lily, "My husband would love to have a little chat with you if you're free later today?"

"Uh, I'd love to but I have so much to do during the day and…"

"I'm sure we can find a quiet moment." Mrs. Riley put a hand on her arm and smiled winningly. "Now I must go and fetch some of the elderly who don't have cars to get here. Excuse me." She turned and made her way back to her car.

Cade stared after her. "I wonder what her husband wants to discuss with you. He's aiming to get reelected next year. Maybe he needs someone for his campaign?"

"I'm not sure I'd have the skills for that. Politics is a different ballgame than business. But thanks for the vote of confidence."

"You did a really great job here and… I missed you while you were away."

Lily stared into Cade's eyes. Had she heard that right? Did he just say he had missed her? A tractor pulled up with a trailer behind it loaded with hay bales. Cade broke eye contact reluctantly and said, "There's Dale with the hay bales. We better discuss how we want them set up."

As Cade helped Dale stack hay bales to form a natural ring around the area for the pig pageant, unrest coursed through his veins. Dakota Riley and her well-meant breakfast had suddenly made him aware of something he had refused to acknowledge earlier. He wanted Lily to stay. Whether it was for the mayor's reelection campaign or something else, any reason that could keep her around. And not for Gina's sake, or because the girls wanted Auntie Lily. No. Because he didn't want her to leave him at a ranch that felt empty without her.

"There." Dale put the last one in place and wiped sweat off his brow. "I'll drive the rig home and come back later for the festivities. How's Gina and the girls?"

"Okay. See you later." Cade turned around and bumped into Lily who had come up with a paper in her hands. They stood shoulders almost touching to look at it.

"I think we're all done now with the layout," she said. "You?" In the same breath she added, "That seemed like a nice man, who helped you with the hay. Did I hear him ask about Gina?"

"Yes." Cade hesitated a moment deciding whether he should say this or not. "But you shouldn't encourage that."

"Sorry?" Lily tilted her head. "Encourage what? How do you mean?"

Cade looked over his shoulder to see if Dale had removed himself out of earshot. "He's a rodeo champ. Always on the circuit, winning prizes. Overly confident, you know the type. As soon as Gina settled back here, Dale found excuses to drop by at the ranch and chat to her. They went to high school together and…had been dating at the time. I don't want to go into details, but he broke her heart. I know it's long ago, but still… Gina has already had enough heartbreak and broken promises in her life. She doesn't need more." It sort of slipped out, but he realized his faux pas as soon as it was spoken. He just hoped that Lily didn't catch on to his meaning.

He walked to his SUV and reached into the back to get the wooden sign Stacey and Ann had painted for the pig pageant. It was a large placard with uneven lettering in bright colors: *Most Beautiful Piggy Ever*, surrounded by hearts and flowers.

When he turned with the thing in his

hands, Lily stood opposite to him. Her expression was tight and her eyes suspicious as she asked, "What do you mean that Gina already had enough heartbreak and broken promises in her life? Do you mean my brother?"

Cade knew he shouldn't engage. He should make up a story, invent a lie to explain. Keep it general and harmless. But his head was empty and he didn't even want to lie. "You have to admit that Barry and Gina differed like day and night. She was a simple country girl and he was a smooth-talking city slicker. She shouldn't even have been on that holiday where they met. Just because a friend of hers fell ill in the last instant, she took her place to go to that fancy all-inclusive resort."

"I know. Gina told me often. She thought their meeting was meant to be."

"Meant to be? Like some movie scenario where the unsuspecting woman gets swept off her feet by the man of her dreams?"

"They were madly in love."

"Maybe. But he took her away from here into an unfamiliar world."

"Don't exaggerate. It's not like Gina had never been to a city before."

"Oh, and Barry didn't think country life beneath him either?" Cade felt anger course through his veins like a wildfire sparking in dry grass and grabbing everything within reach. "Tell me one thing then. Why did they never come to visit us for Thanksgiving and Christmas? Ma invited them every single time. Handmade invitation cards, calls to ask if they had received them. When she got another weak excuse about already having made other commitments, 'so sorry, some other time,' she put the phone down with tears in her eyes. I saw that, even if she'd never say she was disappointed. Never a bad word about Barry. Gina and Barry were married for seven years and how often have they been here during that time? How often do you think?"

"I don't know." Lily looked a bit uncertain now. "I guess they couldn't make every birthday as it was quite a distance but…"

"They have been over maybe four times?" Cade leaned closer to her. "Four times in seven years. What do you think that was like for my mother? Oh, she always said it wasn't a big deal and she could go to them, to see the grandkids. But it became painful listening to those excuses about the pizzeria and engagements with friends and your parents having asked first. I knew what they were. Lies."

Lily cringed under the word, but Cade repeated, "Lies they were, just because they wouldn't tell us to our face what the truth was. That Barry felt too good to come here. He had risen high above us and the simple lifestyle here. He had money and he took his family yachting and skiing and whatnot and we couldn't fit in. Or keep up. We didn't have the money."

He had to pause a moment to breathe. The anger raged through him, burning him head to toe. "But you know what is the worst of all? Barry didn't have the money either. At least we were honest that we couldn't afford it. But he pretended that he could. He got into all that debt, he endangered his family, for what? Luxury travel, new cars, a much too big house. He wanted it all and then when he died, Gina and the kids were out in the street with nothing but the clothes on their backs. They lost everything because of him. Their home, the place where they felt safe. They lost their dignity because they were suddenly hunted by debtors and…" Cade felt a burn behind his eyes. "They came here like they were on the run. All because Barry always wanted more. And then you wonder why I don't want Gina to get anywhere near a guy like that?"

"But you don't ask for Gina's opinion. You don't ask her if she likes to have a chat with Dale. Just a friendly chat, not a date. And even if she wanted to date him, it would be none of your business. Like it wasn't when she met Barry. I know Gina well. She fell in love and she wanted to be with Barry. It was her choice. They were happy."

"So you agree with him getting into debt?"

"That's not the point. You're using the debts to prove in hindsight that Gina should never have married Barry. But their marriage was not a mistake. My brother wasn't someone who only cared for money. He bought his wife and kids the world because he loved them."

"If you really believe that, we have very different views of what love is. Now excuse me because I have to give this sign a good place." He walked away.

LILY STOOD AND stared at Cade's back as the distance between them grew. Very different views of love, he had said. So it was about love, really.

Cade loved Gina and the girls. With all of his heart. It was understandable he was hurt and angry about what had happened to them. And that he had vowed he'd protect them from new hurt. But in doing so he was taking all agency away from them, making decisions for them.

She ran after him and grabbed his arm. "Hey. You say you don't want Gina near a guy like Dale. But that is hardly your decision to make. Gina is a grown woman, with her own family. She's living in your house for the time being but she doesn't have to live by your rules."

"You don't know Dale or what he did to her before."

"*Before*, yes, but today is today. Can't he have changed?"

"You don't know that."

"But you don't either. You're acting on some knee-jerk response rooted in the past. Can't we let the past be the past? Can't we give people a chance? Can't we…give each other a chance? I know you're different from what I first thought about you. And hopefully, you know by now I'm different too. Because of my actions."

CADE HESITATED. The anger was still buzzing in his veins and it was hard to embrace the reasonable approach she suggested. Still he couldn't deny she had surprised him often. That her actions had shown him a kind and loyal heart. That she had been true to her word, reliable and hardworking. That she…

Had become more important to him than he liked to admit?

Lily's fingers put a tender pressure on his arm. She smiled as she said, "Let's go into today open-minded and have fun. It's just for a day."

Those last words were like a door snapping shut on a beautiful vista he was just about to explore. Just for a day, huh? Yes, after this was over, she'd leave again, back to the city, to her life there, to the dream job she wanted. She'd go. Like Gina had gone, and April. Leaving the ranch so quiet and empty without their laughter.

He gritted his teeth to be able to speak without giving anything away. "Sure, for a single day...that shouldn't be so hard."

"Great. You go find a place for that sign the twins worked so hard on and I'll welcome those people." She pointed to a car approaching.

He watched her walk away, her hair bouncing on her shoulders. *You look gorgeous in that dress.*

CHAPTER TWELVE

WHEN EVERYONE WAS busy setting up their booths, and it was still an hour until the official opening, Lily went back to the ranch to see how Gina and Mrs. Williams were doing, getting the girls ready for departure. Cade would follow to help with transporting the animals for the petting zoo. She had barely entered the house when Stacey stood in front of her smiling up at her. "I put on my dress myself. Can you do my hair? I want two braids."

"Of course, honey." Lily took Stacey into the kitchen and put her on a stool so she could easily do her hair. She brushed it, divided it in two halves and began braiding the right-hand side. Rosie sat beside the stool looking at the proceedings with tilted head.

Stacey said, "Today is a very special day, right? We want to try apple fritters. And do a pony ride."

"You first have to ask your mom what you can do, okay? Don't roam around and get her all worried about you. It isn't a huge fair but with all those booths you could get a little lost. Always stay with Grandma or Mom. And look after Ann a bit?" Lily patted Stacey on the shoulder. "You're the bravest."

Stacey said, "Uncle Cade said I shouldn't always get into trouble."

"When was that?"

"Last night. I didn't mean to get him angry. I wasn't doing anything. He also said that you'll be leaving again soon." She knotted her hands. "Is that true?"

The sadness in the little girl's eyes tore at Lily's heart. "You know I live in Denver now. I'm only here to help out with the Apple Fest."

"But you have to play with us. Mommy has to take it easy all of the time because of the baby."

"Once the baby is born, it will be different. And we can still see each other. I can come over for a weekend."

"No, you have to stay. We need you." Stacey pressed her head against Lily.

She wrapped her arms around the little girl. Was she even sure she wanted to leave? Before she had come here, Denver had seemed so attractive. But here she experienced community and family, was close to her beloved rescue pets again.

And there was Cade…

"Please?" Stacey pleaded.

Mrs. Williams came in. "Ah, Lily, you got Stacey ready. Thanks. I'm just done with Ann. I didn't want Gina to tire herself before the big event even begins. Is that Cade to get the animals?"

Lily looked out of the window where Cade's SUV was parking. "I'll go and help him." She rushed out and made a beeline for Cade who was heading for the barn. "Wait a sec. I want to talk to you."

He turned to her. There was a weariness in his features that caught her off guard. He always seemed so strong and in charge. But did he also need others? Did he actually need her?

But he had told Stacey she was leaving. Why say that to a child and make her sad at the prospect of saying goodbye? Couldn't he wait for her to leave and things to return to normal again? She almost shook her head at her own confusing thoughts.

Cade asked with a frown, "Is something the matter? Is Gina not well? Or did Stacey cause trouble? She was getting overexcited about today."

"No, she was rather thoughtful. Seems you told her not to get into trouble all the time." As she repeated Stacey's words, it hit her that this was another example of how he tried to run Gina's life. If he was concerned about the girls' behavior, he should discuss it with Gina and have her talk to them. As their mother she had a gentler touch.

"What did Stacey tell you exactly?" Cade asked, his frown deepening. "Did she tell you I caught her climbing into the hayloft? Did she tell you that if she had fallen down from up there she could have broken her back? Did she tell you that when I told her, very kindly, not to do that again, she told me to my face that she wasn't going to listen to me? That she was going to climb up there because Daddy had said that if you got higher, you were closer to heaven."

Lily stood and stared at him. "What?"

"She didn't want to listen and she almost hurt herself because of that. I said to her that maybe her father had said that, but he would never have wanted his little girl to get hurt. I told her that he would never want her to be irresponsible because it would also make Mommy and Grandma very sad. Now if she told you some other story, she was either twisting the truth because she was worried what you'd say if you heard about her antics, or she genuinely didn't understand what I tried to say to her. It could be either. I don't know." Cade took a deep breath. "I don't always know what to say to them when they're upset about their father, you know. I lost mine when I was twenty-two and I've never hurt so bad in my life. So I can't imagine how it feels when you're only five."

Lily felt her annoyance deflate. Why had she readily assumed he was doing it from a sense of entitlement? He was struggling to help these little girls as much as they all were. It was hard and sometimes there didn't seem to be a right thing to say. "I'm sorry."

"You don't have to be sorry. I just wanted

you to understand how it happened. I still can't work out why Stacey wouldn't listen when I told her to stay away from the hay-loft because it's dangerous."

Lily swallowed hard. "Because she wants to be closer to heaven. To where her daddy is now." She looked up at him. "Gina had to explain to the children where their daddy had gone to. She told them that he went away, to heaven. That it was a beautiful place higher than the mountains with a great view. Stacey said…" She swallowed again because it hurt to recall what Gina had told her. "That Daddy had always liked nice views and that he had to be happy up there. That she only wished…he had taken her with him so they could see it together."

A tear dripped down her cheek. Cade didn't speak. It was silent around them except for the faraway sounds of the animals scurrying in the barn.

Lily said softly, "I think Stacey just wants to be with her daddy."

Cade cleared his throat before he spoke. "I didn't know that. And I'm sorry. I only wanted to prevent her from hurting herself. I was worried she'd do something when our backs were turned and… Gina has been through enough already. She'd blame herself if one of the girls got injured."

"And you'd blame yourself too," Lily said looking up at him. The pain in his deep blue eyes hurt. "You're constantly telling me about all the things that went wrong because of other people's choices, but deep down inside you feel responsible. You think that you should have prevented Gina's unhappiness, somehow. Maybe also April leaving? Or even your father's death? Because you weren't there when it happened?"

Cade's jaw set. "My father was in good health. No one knew he was going to have a heart attack. It was no one's fault. And no one could have prevented it."

It sounded like something he had repeated over and over, to himself.

"That's right," she said softly. "You can't know everything in advance. And you don't have to. People make choices to follow their dreams. Gina loved Barry and April wanted to work on a cruise ship. You have to let them go into the unknown."

"I know," Cade said. "You've made that

very clear to me." He forced a smile. "We'd better get those animals loaded into their trailer or we'll be late."

CHAPTER THIRTEEN

"THERE YOU ARE!" Bud Travers, dressed in a jean jacket with embroidered apples, came over and shook their hands. "The jury for our pig beauty contest. We have some amazing contenders. Why don't you come over and have a look at the participants before we get to the official part of the proceedings?"

Without waiting for their reply he ushered them over to the area behind the makeshift hay bale corral. There a boy of about eleven stood with a large pig on a leash. He rubbed its back and the animal closed its eyes in satisfaction. Two girls held a basket between them in which a potbellied pig sat watching everything with interest. A farmer in blue overalls watched over a large sow while another stood at his pickup with the pig in the back. "A very broad field," Bud Travers said with satisfaction. "I think we can safely say we have a winner among them."

"And for us it will be very hard to make a choice," Cade whispered to Lily. "Because we have no idea what criteria to use. Just look at them."

"They're all beautiful in their own way," Lily agreed.

She walked over to the two girls and asked what the name of their pig was. "Jerry," the eldest girl said. "He can run very fast. He makes funny sounds and he's great to cuddle with. But we always have to treat him with respect and not like a teddy bear."

"That's very good. Hey, Jerry." Lily leaned down to pat the pig on his back. He looked up at her and grunted.

Cade stood talking to the farmer at the pickup, gesturing with his free hand. He had donned his Stetson and with his blue shirt and stonewashed jeans he was the perfect picture of a cowboy. She snapped a photo of him with her cell phone. She wanted lots of photos to use for her project. Of course there was press coming over so there'd also be photos appearing in print and online but she'd rather have her own material to use.

"No, Jerry, no," one of the girls cried and Lily looked down at the basket to see Jerry's little curly tail bob as he jumped out and raced away. He zigzagged between people, dove through a man's legs and avoided a dog who barked at him.

Cade had also noticed the escape and started a pursuit. It was funny to see the tall cowboy race after the pig and try to reach for him. Jerry stopped at a booth with apples where apparently one had landed in the grass. His snout moved over the ground as he looked for a treat. Cade snuck up, his hands poised to grab the small body. But in the last instant the pig noticed the danger and raced ahead, leaving Cade to clutch at thin air.

Lily made a detour around two booths to approach the pig from the other side. She tried to deduce from his movements what he planned next so she could be there ahead of him. Oh, he had smelled the fritters now. He was heading straight for that stall. She saw Cade closing in from the other direction. *If we both keep a side covered, we have to be able to...*

They drew closer. The pig was completely entranced by the food smells. Cade reached down, his fingers spread wide. Lily snuck up from the other side, her arms open, ready to strike. As if they had agreed on it, they both sprang forward.

The pig gave a startled honk and shot under the booth's curtained front. The woman on the other side screamed and dropped the fritter she was frying. Cade and Lily collided, his hand closing around her wrist, her hand closing round his ankle. They fell sideward in a tangle of limbs. People laughed. The two girls who had followed them anxiously called for Jerry as the rampant pig continued on his way across the fairground.

Cade sat up in the grass, his Stetson had fallen away and he rubbed his forehead with a sheepish expression. "I will never ever allow a pig pageant again," he muttered.

Lily said, "I agreed to it in the first place. I'm sorry."

They looked each other in the eye and

then Cade began to laugh. The warm sound reverberated in the air. Lily also burst into giggles. She tried to get up, but she couldn't. They sat in the grass laughing until tears formed in their eyes. Then Cade scrambled to stand and reached out to pull her to her feet. As they stood, close together, Lily staring up into his eyes, she was suddenly conscious of every sound and smell and sight. Music and laughter, crushed grass and caramelized apples. The vanilla of Cade's aftershave. The colors of bunting and people's clothing, the sparkle of the sun on everything around. And the warmth in his eyes as he steadied her. For one single moment the world was perfect and everything was aligned as it should be. In harmony. At peace.

Then someone cried, "Hey look out," and they were reminded of their little fugitive.

"We need a change of tactics," Cade said. "As long as we chase him, he'll keep running. We have to lure him to us." He asked the woman who was baking the fritters for an apple and headed to where the pig was sniffing in the grass. He rolled the apple to him. Jerry saw it and his beady eyes lit. He began to nibble on it. One of the girls came from behind, the basket in her hand. She sat on her haunches and reached out, scooping Jerry up and returning him to his basket. He settled into it chewing with a satisfied grunt.

"He likes to be naughty," the girl declared. "But he's really very sweet."

"Very," Cade said, wiping the sweat off his brow. But his eyes twinkled and Lily thought that they would never have laughed so hard without their little Houdini.

"SO WHAT DO you think?" Cade asked Lily after the pig pageant was over and the sow had been crowned queen of the ball. "We should be getting about ready for our performance with Wayne. Have you already seen him?" He tried to sound casual while he knew very well that Lily had talked to Wayne half an hour ago. From a distance he had watched them with a hawk's eye, searching for clues in their behavior that they were feeling…well, different around each other. But Wayne had looked like his usual jovial self and Lily was always pretty and friendly and social so…there hadn't been much to deduce. Gina had probably just been fantasizing about a relationship between those two as a reason for Lily to stay around here.

Now he wouldn't mind Lily staying around here. But not for Wayne.

"He said he had a special surprise for the performance," Lily said. "We should meet him ten minutes before it starts in the big white tent."

Cade frowned. "Okay. Then we'd better go over and see what it is." He followed Lily who smiled and greeted people as she made her way to the tent. Everyone seemed to know her or want to say something to her. It was great that her efforts for the community were so much appreciated. It seemed to him that she was at home here. But then he didn't know if she was like this all the time. Maybe she just engaged easily with strangers?

At the tent Lily peeked in. "Hey, Wayne. Can we come in?" Cade followed her as she held up the flap for him to enter.

Wayne stood beside a chest in the back. He held up a white jacket with gold stitching. "I got these costumes. Jackets for us and a dress for Lily. I asked Gina what size to get. Have a look."

Cade leaned back on his heels. "Do we really have to dress up?"

"That's fun." Lily accepted the dress Wade handed her. "Look how it sparkles."

It was white and fell just over the knee with golden sequins on the top, short sleeves and hemline. Lily said, "I'll try it on right away. You wait outside."

Cade and Wayne dutifully stepped out. Cade guarded the tent's entrance like a watchdog so no careless local could barge in on Lily.

Wayne said, "So you two are really hitting it off, right?"

"How do you mean?"

"Come on. The way you look at her…"

Cade felt his neck heat. "Funny you should say that. Gina is convinced *you* are interested in Lily." He wanted to add a probing, "Are you?" But he knew Wayne wouldn't be serious about it, and it might only arouse more suspicion. Apparently Wayne had seen something special already. *The way you look at her.*

"Well, you can't blame me if I like being around her." Wayne grinned at him. "She's a cute little thing."

"Just don't go flirting with Lily and then breaking her heart. She's been through enough recently with her brother passing away and all. She had to move, start a new job."

"Feeling a touch protective?" Wayne asked, eyes sparkling.

"Just explaining the circumstances. She's Gina's best friend and if you do anything to hurt her, I'll…"

"Whoa, last time we fought over a girl was in the kindergarten sandbox." Wayne seemed determined not to be serious. "You paint Lily's life to me like she's a weeping willow while I see a woman who lives life to the fullest and isn't afraid of a challenge."

"Being your girlfriend would be a challenge," Cade said.

"I'm ready," Lily's voice called from within. "Come and have a look whether I can actually show myself to people like this."

Wayne opened the flap and stepped

in. Cade heard him whistle. He followed quickly.

Lily stood in the middle of the tent in the dress, her long hair loose over her shoulders. It framed her face that beamed with happiness. The sequins flashed like lines of fire as she moved her shoulders and then swirled round. "What do you think?"

Cade's head was empty. Just totally, completely blackout empty. All he could do was stare. He heard Wayne say something about a beautiful lady and then he even kissed her hand.

Cade knew he should say or do something, if only he could remember what. He muttered something about getting ready for the performance and then left the tent.

LILY INHALED SHARPLY as the flap fell to a close. It was nice Wayne enthused about her outfit but she had wanted to hear Cade's opinion. Earlier she might have thought he was angry his friend had rented these costumes without discussing it with them first. Or even that he thought she looked ridiculous and didn't want to perform beside her. But now she wondered if he also felt the attraction between them that she did and didn't know how to deal with it.

"Where is he going?" Wayne asked. "You stay put. People can't see you yet. It will spoil the entire surprise of the performance. I'll go and fetch Cade. Just like him to play Mr. Grumpy and ruin the thing. Wait here. Promise me you won't sneak out."

"I promise."

She knotted her fingers as Wayne vanished to retrieve Cade. She couldn't deny that there was something between her and Cade or that it complicated the situation. After all, he was firmly rooted here and she was destined for Denver. The point of this whole day was to pave the way for her permanent position at the firm. So no matter how good a time they had, everything was tinged with a hint of goodbye. And where Stacey already hadn't bought into her nice promise of stopping by sometime, Cade certainly wouldn't. He knew how those things turned out. She couldn't have both the job and Cade. And for her the job was winning. She had worked so hard for it; she needed to feel proud of herself again. And make her parents proud of her.

She wasn't about to sacrifice that for a budding feeling, a tenderness inside that didn't even make sense. Because Cade might feel attracted to her, but he didn't want emotional connections. He wanted to do everything by himself.

Cade stumbled into the tent. Wayne's voice sounded from the outside. "Now talk it over and get ready and I'll check out the podium. Five minutes to showtime."

"I think it's minus five minutes already," Cade said with a sour look. "Sorry but…"

Lily walked over and put her hand on his arm. "Cade, if you hate the idea of performing with us, Wayne and I can do it together. I understand that you have a certain image to uphold in the district, people know you as a serious guy."

"Who just chased a pig." Cade's mouth twitched in a self-deprecating smile.

"But I don't want you to feel embarrassed."

Cade stared into her eyes. "Embarrassed?" he echoed. "How could I ever feel embarrassed to be seen with you? In that dress…" He let his gaze wander over her expression as if he couldn't find the right words. "You look different than I've ever seen you before. I just have to get used to it. Or maybe I won't."

She frowned, unsure what he meant. "Do I need to change or not? Time is running out."

"No, don't change." He put his hand on her shoulder. "Don't change in any way, Lily. You're perfect the way you are and…"

She stood motionless as his face came closer to hers. As she drowned in his blue eyes, savored his nearness. There was such warmth in those eyes and longing. She waited for his lips to touch hers and…

"Ready, guys?" Wayne's voice resounded. "Grab your stuff, we're on!"

Cade broke away from her and scrambled to get into his jacket and get his guitar. Lily smoothed down her dress one more time, checked her hair and went to the tent's exit. Her heart hammered hard. She couldn't make sense of what had just happened. She had almost kissed Cade. Or in any case she had felt like he was about to kiss her. It shouldn't surprise her as she had known the attraction was there, but she hadn't thought he would act on it. He was so aware she was leaving. And he didn't want a long-distance relationship.

Her heartbeat fluttered and her thoughts scattered through her head like birds driven into flight. He had said something about... her being perfect the way she was and... Earlier he had said he had never met anyone like her. What was happening to them? Was it just the beautiful day, the nerves before the performance?

Yes, nothing but nerves. She had to take a deep breath and try to be herself again. Grab that microphone and rock the performance. In honor of Apple Fest and all those people who had gathered to celebrate the community, friendship and standing together in times of need.

CADE STOOD ON the platform and went through the familiar motions of swinging his guitar, belting the silly song Wayne had composed about apples and festivities, and tried not to look too much at Lily. He was worried that if he made eye contact with her, he'd forget his lines.

Not that anyone would notice as Wayne was singing so loud. He obviously relished the return of the Heartmont Heroes and made the most of his moment in the spotlight, flirting with the ladies in the front row whether they were twenty or seventy. He swung his hips, winked and gave melting looks while the crowd went wild.

Cade was happy to hang back and wished it would be over soon. It was bittersweet reminding him of all those other times when he had performed here and his father had still been alive, sitting in his booth doing his wood engraving. Ma had sold apple products, Gina had played with her friends and April had created her own little business selling the felt apple key chains she made to save to buy her own pony. He had thought they'd always be that way: together, happy.

But it had turned out so differently. Dad was gone, Ma had worries, Gina was a widow, April had decided she wanted to be a cruise attendant and traveled the seven seas. Their whole family had fallen apart. On a day like this he felt that more than ever.

But he also saw something else, clearly. No matter who was no longer there, the three of them were here. Wayne and him and Lily. They played songs, they laughed and looked toward the future. They carried on, despite their losses. There were good things ahead. Because of Lily's insistence to do something for them, organize this day and bring everyone together again.

Wayne ended the song with a vigorous guitar solo and everyone cheered. Lily stepped back, her cheeks red, and looked over her shoulder at Cade. The moment their gazes locked, something twisted in his stomach. It was an unfamiliar feeling, something from too long ago, almost forgotten but suddenly alive and raising a hundred questions.

Lily bowed as the crowd cried for an encore. Lily looked at Wayne and he gestured to her to stand ready. He mouthed something to her then to Cade. What was that? "Achy Breaky Heart"?

Of course. One of Wayne's classics. They played and the crowd sang along, men wrapping their arms around their wives, kids joining hands to dance in circles. Everyone was swaying, singing, tapping their feet to the rhythm. From the platform Cade looked out over a sea of cheerful people losing themselves in the music. It felt good to stand here again and contribute to the community. More than he usually did. Work behind the scenes, newsletters and meetings and… It could become impersonal. But here were the people he worked for right in front of him, his neighbors and friends waving at him. Cheering him, and Wayne and Lily.

They stood and enjoyed the thunderous applause. Wayne joined hands with Lily for a bow and Cade had to come stand beside her as well. When her fingers slipped in his palm, a jolt of electricity passed through his arm straight into his chest. It had to be the adrenaline of their performance, the emotion of being united on this special day. The underlying memories of so many earlier Apple Fests when Dad had still been alive. He just had to smile through it and then later things would return to normal again.

LILY CAST A look at Cade's expression. He seemed a bit dazed. Maybe he hadn't expected the audience to like their music as much? Or was he overwhelmed by the sudden feeling of connection? Music had this power to touch the heart. Some spectators were also wiping away tears, perhaps thinking of their crops that had been damaged or their prospects for the future after the storm. But here they were, standing together to raise money and ensure that their beautiful community would continue.

She pressed Cade's hand to let him know she felt for him. He looked at her and there was something deep in his eyes she couldn't quite define. Protectiveness? Tenderness? Something more than just a spark of attraction.

The moment when he had almost kissed her came back to her and made her breathing grow shallow. She had wanted him to kiss her. It hadn't happened, but she had wanted him to. If Wayne hadn't interrupted, she might have reached up to touch Cade's cheek and closed the distance herself, putting her lips to his.

That meant trouble. The last thing she wanted was to fall in love. She wanted to focus on work. Not be distracted by feelings that made so little sense. Cade and she had started off as polar opposites and she wasn't going to believe they suddenly had things in common.

She pulled her hand free and waved at the crowd. She had to stay in character, a country star who was here performing, smiling at the adoring fans. She had to be someone other than Lily Roberts. Because the real Lily Roberts was down-to-earth and practical and realistic and wouldn't dream of kissing a cowboy she barely knew. She would understand it was impossible to have any kind of relationship with someone rooted in a small town away from Denver where her own future lay. She had to remind herself of that over and over, to make sure her silly heart stopped making leaps whenever he looked into her eyes. It wouldn't be that hard. Just stay firm today. Then her task here was over and she could leave. Run away from the confusing feelings and back to the sensible choices she had made.

They walked to the edge of the platform where a few makeshift steps led down. Wayne jumped off, leaned his guitar against the side of the platform and reached up to help Lily. She wanted to put her hand in his, but he gripped her waist and lifted her off, swinging her through the air. The crowd roared and Lily flushed.

Wayne put her down with a grin. "You're a true star. We should think about a continuation of this. A tour maybe?" He winked.

Cade said, "This was a onetime occasion. And mind your guitar. It could fall over and break."

Wayne picked it up and grinned at Lily. "Let me know if you want to get famous." He sauntered off and a group of girls followed asking for a selfie with him.

"He's just weird. You shouldn't take him seriously," Cade said to Lily.

"But it was fun, wasn't it?" She smiled up at him. "I've never done anything quite like it." And she had certainly never felt this way.

CADE HELD HER GAZE. She had such gorgeous radiant eyes. They bubbled with life and laughter. But was she merely happy because she had done this great performance?

No, back in the tent she had been about to kiss him.

If they had only had a few more seconds, then it would have been too late to turn back. They would have kissed and the kiss would have told her everything he couldn't put into words.

But they hadn't kissed.

Not yet. "Um, what about a little tour of the fairground? I don't think you've seen the mobile apple press yet."

"No, what is that?"

He started explaining, rather badly, that it was a machine to press apples on the spot. People could buy the freshly pressed juice per cup to drink right away or per gallon to take home. They were walking in the direction when he recalled he was still dressed up and carrying his guitar. He should have suggested they get changed first but it was too late for that. He already saw the press and people crowding round it to buy juice. He asked if Lily wanted some and then told her to wait there while he got it.

He waited his turn, glancing back at her. She stood looking around her with a warm and excited expression. This was the result of her hard work and she was clearly proud of it. A man with a large camera on his neck and a lady in a pantsuit with a microphone approached. The lady stood beside Lily while the man filmed their conversation. Lily explained something, gesturing around her. She was immediately businesslike, apparently sharing information about the fair and the reasons why it had been organized. He collected his two cups of apple juice and waited a little nearer to them until she was done.

He caught her saying something about the community having pulled together to organize this and the ranchers being committed to bring more tourists to the area for the long run, by setting up a newsletter and selling more home produce, having a ranch open house or sharing on social media. She mentioned links and the page to get a newsletter subscription. After the camera stopped filming, the woman said, "Thanks for the information, we can run the links in the bottom of the screen for people to contact you if they want to. This is really well organized on short notice."

"Oh well, I had a wonderful template to work from. Apple Fest has been celebrated here for decades. It was the brainchild of a lovely couple who worked on it until the wife died. Then it became more difficult for the husband to keep it all running. But we are now determined to revive it. This is just a single-day event to show what we can do and to raise money to repair the storm damage. But we will continue the yearly tradition of the Apple Fest in October with several weekends of activities."

We, she said. We. As if she was part of this and intended to…stay?

Cade clenched the cups tighter. No. He shouldn't fantasize. Lily was leaving. She had organized everything because she wanted to leave. Because her life, her future was in Denver. If he had any sense at all, he wouldn't kiss her. Because it could only end in heartbreak. She'd have to choose between him and her job and… Aside from what her choice might be he didn't even want her to choose. It was obvious what she should do. She had said it herself. People had to chase their dreams. She was chasing hers and he had to let her.

She said goodbye to the reporter and came over to him. "Ah, thanks." She reached for the cup. "I can use a cool drink. My throat is dry from all the singing."

Her fingers brushed his and again he felt a sort of jolt. He wanted to ask her what she had meant about we and us, if the town meant anything to her, life here. She did fit in, he saw that with his own eyes. Could he plead with her to see it too?

He almost shook his head to get himself back to reality. It wasn't fair. Lily had done enough for them. For Gina and the girls, the ranch, the community. After today, she had earned her reward. She had to get that job, also to appease her parents who were pressuring her to come and work for them at the resort. She had made it very clear to him she didn't want that. She wanted to earn recognition on her own, feel good about herself. And she deserved that.

"Why the frown?" she asked. "Aren't you happy with the way things are going? They feel kind of good to me."

"Oh yeah, great. I'm just uh…thinking of what's still to come. I have to do some more engraving, then see that the BBQ food doesn't run out and the man who does the fireworks at the end of the night will pull in later to get set up."

"But you can't get all wrapped up in your to-do list," she said with earnest concern. "You also have to enjoy today. This is for you too." She held his gaze as she said, "We revived Apple Fest for the entire community of course and to help out after the storm, but…when we decided on it, I also secretly hoped it would bring you back to the days of old when you had fun as a family here and…when your father was still alive."

Cade felt a stab of pain inside and at the same time a sort of peaceful feeling that Dad would have loved this and it was good they had done it. "He would have liked to know you," he said to Lily. "I think the two of you would have gotten along really well."

"You think so? Why?"

"He enjoyed being creative, making things with his hands and you're just the same in your work. He would have appreciated your imagination."

Lily made a dismissive gesture. "It's not a big deal."

"But it is. You throw yourself into everything you do with zeal. You commit wholeheartedly. You even dressed up like a country star to do a performance with us."

Lily grinned and fingered her costume. "I even felt like a country star. A true Dolly Parton for the day."

For the day.

Yes, he had to remember that. This was just one day. Away from real life. Doing unusual things and feeling unusual feelings. Tomorrow it would be back to normal again. They'd have work to do, promises to keep. Lily was here now embracing their country ways, but that was like putting on that dress she wore. It was a costume for a dress-up moment. Not what she felt comfortable in or what she'd choose for herself.

He had to keep that in mind as he showed her around.

She toasted him with her apple juice cup. "To a wonderful day, Cade."

He touched his cup to hers. "To a wonderful day."

CHAPTER FOURTEEN

THE SCENT OF grilling was still in the air but most people had finished eating and were dancing to the music of the three-man live band. They played their fiddles and guitar with energy, encouraging the crowd to clap along. Wayne had swirled Lily onto the dance floor and was now doing a sort of rock and roll dance, pushing her away from him, then pulling her closer again. Lily dissolved into giggles every other movement and Wayne's funny faces as he danced didn't help. Gasping for breath, she gestured at him to stop and Wayne bowed to her and thanked her before he turned to a woman standing on the sidelines and invited her to join him for a mad roundabout.

Lily staggered over to a hay bale and sank onto it to catch her breath. She raked her hair back from her warm face as she watched the couples dance. Even little children turned in circles, laughing as they lost their balance and tumbled in the grass. Overhead the sky was turning dark blue as the sun set and the first stars appeared. It had been a great day.

"Hey." Cade came to sit beside her. Although his shoulder didn't touch hers, she immediately felt his warmth reaching out to her. She had been distracted by the dancing, but suddenly reunited she realized she had missed him. Somehow Cade's presence made things complete.

"I didn't see you for a bit." She studied his profile. "Don't you dance?"

"Oh, I dance but... I was busy checking with various people to hear how they did. I mean, I thought it would be nice to know how much we raised today. I haven't got all the numbers together so I can't name a definite amount, but with the fundraising page you opened online, we're past ten thousand dollars."

"That's wonderful."

"Of course we can't repair all the damage with that amount, but the people I talked to all said that the tourists who were here today were very interested in their

products and crafts and took along contact information to get in touch again later.
So I have high hopes that we can actually
achieve more tourism to the town and the
individual businesses. Also because of the
newsletter you put together and the media
attention you got. Look here..." He pulled
out his phone and scrolled for a minute,
then showed her a video. Lily saw herself
talking to the lady who had interviewed
her. She immediately noticed with a critical eye that her hair was a little unkempt
and that she gestured too much with her
hands. But Cade didn't seem to notice. He
stared at the screen as if mesmerized and
when the clip had ended, he said, "You did
amazing, just like a professional."

"Well, I should hope so. Promoting stuff
is my work, you know."

Cade pocketed the phone again. He
rubbed his hands together a moment as if
he was uncomfortable. The band started
playing a slow song. Lily saw Stacey and
Ann running to Gina who sat in a plastic
chair with her feet up on a stool. She cuddled the girls and brushed their cheeks. It

was lovely to see her here embedded in the community.

"Do you want to dance?" Cade asked. Lily turned her head to look at him. His blue eyes seemed darker now, changing like the skies above. He gave her that probing look as if he wanted to see deep inside her and determine if she really wanted to dance with him.

She had already danced with the mayor, the sheriff, Bud Travers and Wayne, so it should be perfectly natural to accept this offer, but as she nodded and rose, it felt suddenly momentous. She had agreed to dance with the others to be sociable on a festive day, but here was the man she truly wanted to dance with. He reached out and she put her hand in his as he led her to the dance floor.

Those brief steps stretched out in time as if she lived it in slow motion. His warm grasp around her hand, the soft grass under her feet, the music playing in the distance. The moment they stopped and stood opposite each other before he lifted her hand and put it against his chest. She involuntarily held her breath. Then she raised her other hand and put it against his chest as well. He wrapped his arms around her waist and they started moving, slowly in tune with the nostalgic music. The people around them were a blur as she only had eyes for him and the look in his eyes as he smiled down on her.

Flashes came back to her of her time out here, first meeting Cade on the land, among his broken flowers and reaching out quite naturally to him to help. Sitting at the dinner table and laughing over pizza, playing with the girls. Working to get the schedule for Apple Fest running. Seeing the look on his face when he had seen her in the sparkling dress for the performance.

They hadn't known each other long, but it seemed that the shared experiences and the highly emotional circumstances of the storm's aftermath had put everything in a pressure cooker, creating a suddenly intense relationship. A bond between them that seemed to overwhelm her as they danced under the stars. Nothing had ever seemed so real as this feeling. Everything else was far away, her Denver dreams. Her belief she didn't need anyone. Right now it felt so right to be in his arms. To dance to the music with him. To be together in this place where she felt like...she belonged?

The music ended on a high note, people broke apart. Lily woke as if from a dream and stood dazed staring up at Cade. A chilly breeze crept across her bare arms and she shivered a moment.

"You should have brought a cardigan," he said. "Let me see if there is something in the SUV." He left her standing, hurrying away, as ever practical and to the point.

Had he even sensed how magical it had been? How good it had felt? Or was this just a friendship thing? Was he kind to her because he was kind to everyone? Was it...

Argh! Her head was so full right now and all she wanted was to quietly savor the moment. See the happy people around her and feel like they were her community. That they shared a common connection to the land and the animals and the Rockies in the distance.

"Here." Cade had returned at top speed and put a fleece jacket around her shoulders. It was his own probably, because it carried his scent. As he wrapped it around her, she realized how much she wanted to be in his arms. To be one of the couples standing around the dance floor watching and chatting and laughing and feeling so safe with each other.

Maybe it was just the silent splendor of that great sky over them. Or the reality of the earth under their feet, earth that fed them with grain and fruit, delighted them with flowers and supported their weight as they danced. Being here in the heart of nature and feeling how awesome it was, how it was part of them and they were part of it. She had never had that in the city. But here she felt it with such an intensity that tears pressed behind her eyes. A sudden sense of wonder she hadn't felt since childhood when she had been at the sea for the very first time collecting shells and watching the seagulls soar up above.

"Not cold anymore?" Cade asked and she shook her head. She wanted to tell him she wouldn't be cold anymore if he wrapped his arm around her, but it would feel a bit odd to ask and besides, she didn't want other people to see it and speculate. So far everyone had just taken it for granted that they worked together, not asking questions about how they had met or... what their connection was. She didn't want to feed the gossip mill.

CADE STOOD BESIDE LILY, watching as the band played a lively tune while a row of women line danced to it. He basked in the quiet sense of having seen these kinds of scenes for all of his life and just feeling at home here. This was his county, his land, his kind of people. He had loved his time at college and he had made friends there, but the city and city life would never be his style. It had a different rhythm to it and he longed for the song of the country. For the scents here, the sounds, the companionship of people who understood when he worried about the harvest or could tell the weather by just looking at the signs in the sky. They were all alike here, even if they were also different. But they had a connection, an unspoken bond.

He had always thought you could only feel it with country people, farmers, ranchers. But now he felt it with Lily. As he looked at her warm face as she lost herself in the dance performance, watched with fire in her cheeks, and her life-hungry eyes, he felt connected to her in a way he had never felt connected to someone else before. It was as if she got him, even without words.

The dance ended and Lily looked up at him. For a moment they just stared at each other, suspended in time. He didn't want to say something and break this connection. She felt it too, he just knew it.

"Hey, pretty." Wayne appeared by their sides and put his hand on Lily's shoulder. "How about one more dance?"

The musicians started playing again and Lily nodded and offered her hand to Wayne. Cade's jacket slipped off her shoulders and he could just catch it as she walked away. Maybe what he imagined to be special between them was just a figment of his imagination? Maybe she was kind and friendly to everyone because she was a guest here. Or because her project had to succeed. And even if the attraction was real, even if she felt it too, she wanted to leave again for Denver. He had to keep that in mind.

He could of course ask her to come back sometime. Spend a weekend. After all, Denver wasn't Australia. But it was about more than distance. It was about goals, about lifestyle. He was kind of a loner. He loved doing things his own way. He was often busy with work. What could he even offer Lily? To sit around on the ranch while he was away working all day long? Not exactly an attractive prospect for her. She had her own ambitions, a clear career path. And she was good at what she did. He wanted her to have that success.

"Are you having a good time?" His mother stood by his side. Something in her eyes made him cautious. Had she watched him and Lily? Had she thought, like Wayne apparently had, that maybe she saw something there? He had to dispel the notion as quickly as he could. "Yeah, everyone is having a great time. It has been a good day for the region. I think we can safely say Apple Fest is alive again."

"Because of Lily." His mother smiled warmly.

"Yes, she did a great job." Cade leaned down to pet Rosie who pressed herself against his legs. She had been with his mother most of the day and now showed him she had missed him. "But then Lily is a professional. I'm sure this project will get her the job she wants so much. She deserves it. That firm is lucky they get to keep her."

His mother blinked as if she suddenly recalled there even was a firm and a job. "Yes," she said hesitantly, "I suppose that Lily is still set on..."

"Certainly. She mentioned it a few times today. How excited she is about showing her boss the end results and all. She will collect links to sites that shared the event and media attention and all for her presentation. I bet that sometime next week she's going back to Denver." As he said it, his throat grew tight. He didn't want her to leave. He didn't want her to start a life far away. But that had been exactly the point. Her work here for the community had been aimed at securing that position. She had mentioned to him how she needed that job. And he believed her.

"I guess I got used to having Lily around," his mother said. "It was good for Gina too. I saw her laughing a lot. And the girls cling to Lily. They adore her."

"I know, but we can't impose on her time. She was generous enough to come here and spend these weeks with us." *It was too short*, his brain repeated, *far too short...*

But at the same time it might be good she was leaving. He was getting far too attached to her. A red warning light blinked in the back of his mind. What he felt was dangerous. It could only lead to disappointment. To heartbreak maybe, even if he allowed himself to think of what she meant to him already. How much it would hurt when she left. He had once vowed to himself never to feel that pain again. Work hard, make yourself useful, keep your feelings out of the equation. Focus on attainable goals. He had been doing that for many years. He could keep doing it. He simply had to forget how good it had felt to have her by his side this day, to share, to receive instead of giving all the time.

But no, the situation was quite clear to him.

He had to keep his emotions out of it. She had come here to help Gina and she had kept her word. She had given her very best for her friend, the ranch, the town. She was now entitled to her success and the job it could bring her. He had to be a good sport about it, be happy for her and… let her go.

CHAPTER FIFTEEN

THE SUV STOPPED in the yard. They had stayed on the terrain longest clearing stuff away. Moving hay bales and picking up errant candy wrappers that had been left in the grass. To buy time. As if neither of them had wanted the day to end.

But maybe she only imagined that because she felt that way? Maybe Cade was just his usual self, hardworking and conscientious. Practical too. What he cleaned up now, needn't be cleaned up tomorrow.

Tomorrow. Lily wished it would never be tomorrow. That it could stay today forever and she'd feel fuzzy and wrapped in the warmth of Cade's nearness and the silly idea that she could be his. That she could stay here and belong.

It had never been her dream to live on a ranch, to work the land, or to be part of a small-town community. But in the past few weeks she had lived that life and it had oddly suited her. An unexpected surprise. A gift.

And a challenge. Because what was it now that she really wanted? Denver and the dream job. Staying with the firm who had graciously offered her a chance while she didn't have a bachelor's degree. She owed them and she loved the work she did there. Her colleagues praised her and with this successful project she might even win skeptical Eva Bailey around. It was her big chance to work in marketing and also show her parents she could achieve something without them giving her a job at the resort. Before she had come here, it had looked like the dream outcome, bringing her everything she had wanted. And she still wanted success, approval, recognition. Why would she give up on all of that, just when it was within reach?

She glanced at Cade who sat a moment after he had turned the ignition off. The outside lamp at the ranch cast a soft light over his profile. She felt like she had known him much longer than just a few weeks. And yet she knew that she didn't know him at all. He was so guarded, always keeping her at arm's length. They had shared emotional moments in which they had felt strongly connected, but right after he could be a stranger again, locking her out. What was he thinking right now? Was he feeling the same way as she did? Did he sense the attraction and struggle with the question of whether they should give in to it?

Part of her wanted him to struggle, hard, and…succumb? The other half thought it was better if he was the sensible one and ensured nothing happened. Then she could leave and…avoid complications. She didn't want to risk her friendship with Gina by falling for her brother. Once they had acknowledged feelings, how could she stay in touch as a casual friend?

Cade opened the car door and got out. He rounded the SUV to her side and opened the door for her. She got out and looked up at the sky. There were so many stars now. "I've never seen so many stars in the city," she observed. "Too much artificial light. It's too bad really. Just look at them."

"It's odd." Cade's voice was close to her, warm and deep. "I'm often out and about in the dark but I don't often take the chance to look up and truly see the stars. I'm always in a hurry to get inside because the alarm clock is set for 6:00 a.m. But now that you point it out to me, I suddenly see again how beautiful the sky really is."

He waited a moment and added, "You've done more than that, Lily. Since you've been here it's like…everything is more alive."

She held her breath as she listened to him, her eyes still on the night sky and those pricks of silvery light against the velvety canopy.

"I suddenly see things I never saw before," he said. "I…feel things I've never felt before."

A shiver went down her spine and goose bumps formed on her arms. Nerves wriggled in her stomach. What was he going to say next? She ached for him to say more, to finally open up and share his heart with her. But she was also afraid of what it would mean. Of the hard choices she'd have to make.

Impossible choices even? What did she truly want? What did she really need?

But Cade didn't say anything. He just put his hand under her chin and lifted her face to him. Their eyes met and she fell into the warmth they radiated to her. He leaned in as he had in the tent when they were dressing for their performance. She had wanted it then and she wanted it now. Even more.

His lips brushed hers very softly, tenderly. Almost reluctantly as if he had forgotten how to do it and had to feel his way back to it, carefully, step by step. She closed her eyes and savored the kiss, his nearness, the reassurance that everything was alright now.

But then he broke away from her and looked at her with his eyes wide, as if he was waking from a dream and grappling with reality. She could understand that. This kiss turned the world upside down, scattered all the pieces of the puzzle she had just fit into a meaningful whole.

Her heart beat fast as if she was doing something incredibly dangerous. Forbidden even? Why allow herself to fall into this feeling? It had been a special day and everything was different than it usually was. Emotions ran high and… Was it even real?

Would she not wake up in the morning and regret it?

"I'm sorry," he said. "I probably shouldn't have done that."

"It's okay," she rushed to say. "I understand."

CADE FROWNED. She understood?

Understood what? That he had kissed her?

That he shouldn't have kissed her?

That it had happened on the spur of the moment and wasn't even real? But it had felt real.

So real that he was still shaking. That he couldn't quite determine what was happening to him. How he could be falling again, and so hard, for someone he hadn't even understood at the start? But he hadn't known her for what she really was. He had been deceived by all these notions...

Oh, had he been deceived then? Or was he deceived now? Into thinking they could actually be together? While they were so different and moving in opposite directions?

"I mean, uh," he said, "it wouldn't be a good idea to get into a relationship with you headed for Denver. You are…still headed for Denver, right?" His heart beat fast at the idea that she might say no, not anymore, I want to stay with you.

"That was the whole point, right?" Lily asked. "I can hardly cancel my project. I worked on it on my boss's time. To prove to her I deserve the job. It would be terribly ungrateful to turn my back on it all. And my parents… They would never understand such a decision."

"This is not about your boss. Or your parents. This is about you. Us." He cleared his throat. "You told me earlier I shouldn't be so hung up on the past. And you were right. What grew between us has nothing to do with Barry or Gina, or whoever else. Just us. You and me. We can decide…"

"No, we can't." Her voice was soft, but her eyes determined. "We've got obligations. You to the ranch, me in the city. It's more than just duty or career. It's something we believe in."

"I agree. But isn't this feeling special? I know it's something I haven't felt for a long time."

"Maybe it's just the long day or the giddiness of dancing," she said. "We both need sleep to rest up and get some distance. A different perspective."

He wanted to say something, but she raised her hand to stop him. "A grip on reality even, Cade. You aren't the type to leap first and think later. And I don't want to make any more mistakes. Let's sleep on it and discuss in the morning, okay?" She gave him a sad smile and rushed off, into the house.

He could understand she was worried about what she felt. It complicated matters in a major way. Why had he even kissed her and started all of this?

But after he had showered and lay on his bed, his hands folded under his head, he couldn't sleep at all. His head was full of images of Lily and of how much he liked to see her and be with her. How he hated for her to leave. And that was exactly the reason why he shouldn't have risked that kiss. Because she might be leaving anyway. What good could a conversation do? If only she was driven by ambition, he might try and show her. But he understood her need to have the career she had dreamed of before her commitment to family had taken it away. She wasn't resentful about it or bitter, she just wanted her chance now that it was there for the taking. How could he ask her to give up on it? To make a sacrifice, again?

CHAPTER SIXTEEN

THE NEXT MORNING Lily stood at the sink cleaning carrots for lunch. She hadn't seen Cade at all. He had been up early to check on the trees. The late varieties still had some apples not knocked off by the storm and like a worried mother Cade checked on their ripening progress every day. Then, just before family breakfast at 8:30, he had left for a friend who had some trouble with his tractor. Apparently Cade was a mechanic too. Someone who had an answer to everything.

Lily didn't know whether to smile or be annoyed. She had risen with a nervy feeling about the conversation he had claimed he wanted them to have. She had felt the need to see him and discover how he responded to her after last night.

But he wasn't even there and... It was typical. He didn't really want to talk, show his innermost thoughts. His mother had said his father had been just like that. Well, fine that she had been able to marry a taciturn man and make a success of it, but Lily didn't see herself doing it. How could she have a deep meaningful relationship with someone who avoided talking about his feelings? Who always hid behind work?

She heard an engine and despite her thoughts, her heart somersaulted. That had to be him. And she knew the instant she looked into his mesmerizing eyes that all her doubts would go out of the window and she would just want to run into his arms and kiss him. If only he said that he cared for her. That they were worth a chance. If only he gave her a reason to consider giving up all she wanted and…

But it was an unfamiliar car that halted. A man in a suit got out and looked at the ranch house. He had a tight, almost angry expression on his face. Lily's stomach clenched with raw nerves. Who was he? What did he want here? Did it have to do with the storm damage? Insurance maybe?

She cleaned her hands on a tea towel and went outside. Rosie wanted to come with her, but she told her to stay inside. She didn't know how the dog would respond to the tension the man exuded. She'd have to brave this storm alone. She pasted her friendliest smile on and tried to put energy into her voice. "Good morning. Can I help you?"

"Are you Ms. Roberts?"

"Yes."

"It's about your debts."

"Oh, I'm sorry. You mean Mrs. Roberts, my sister-in-law." Lily's throat was so tight she could hardly swallow. "I'll go and get her. She's in the barn with her little girls."

"You better take care of those children for the time being." The man looked grim. "I have some unpleasant news to share."

"I see. One moment please."

Lily walked to the barn. Her legs were rubbery and she felt like she needed support to get there. She opened the door. Gina stood at the stall where Millie and Mollie were being brushed by the girls. They laughed and chatted. Her heart broke for this little family that had already endured so much and was about to be rocked on a new wave of trouble.

"Gina, can you step out a moment? There is someone to see you."

Gina turned to her and came over, smiling, unsuspecting.

Lily whispered, "It's a man in a suit. He said it's about the debts. He doesn't look very…accommodating."

"Oh." Gina paled.

Lily wanted to wrap an arm around her and shield her against the bad news. But she couldn't. Gina had to find out what it was about and then they'd talk it over and find a solution. Somehow. "I'll look after the girls. You go and see him. Just be brave. Don't agree to anything until you've seen paperwork okay?"

Gina nodded. "I know the drill." She walked to the door, her hands shaking. Lily felt so sorry for her.

"Where is Mommy going?" Ann asked. Her voice trembled with suspicion.

"She has a visitor." Lily forced a wide smile. "We're going to make Millie and Mollie really pretty. Go on, that's right." She encouraged the girls for a few minutes and then when they were occupied, went to the door to peek out. Gina and the man stood at his car. Apparently he hadn't wanted to come into the house. Or had Gina not even asked him? She was tomato red now and held a paper in her hand that she was looking at as if it was on fire.

New debts? More difficulties? What could it be?

Lily saw the man get into his car. He started the engine and drove off. Gina remained standing as if rooted to the ground.

"I put something on the stove for lunch," Lily lied to the girls. "I have to go and see that it doesn't burn. You go to Grandma in the other barn, okay?" She accompanied them to the door of the second barn and once they were inside, their voices chatting happily to their grandmother, she closed the door and hurried over to Gina. As she reached her, tears were running down Gina's face. She held the paper out to Lily. "There are new debts. I don't know where they found them but... They say Barry took out another line of credit or something. It's a huge amount. I said I didn't have anything left, that I'm living with my widowed mother again. How will Ma respond when she hears this? And Cade... He vowed he'd help me. He'll never accept he can't. He'll take another mortgage on the ranch or whatnot, and then it's my fault if they get in financial trouble too."

With pounding heart Lily looked over the paper. The figures, the threatening language made her head spin. But one thing was crystal clear to her. She had to make sure Cade didn't indebt himself to solve this. The ranch should never suffer for this. Barry's spending, his debts, had ruined enough. It had cost Gina her house, it had cost their parents the pizzeria. It shouldn't take any more.

"Listen." She put her hands on Gina's shoulders and smiled at her. "I know Cade promised you he'd help you. And he meant it. But sometimes you can't solve things on your own. I protected Barry for years, hiding his mistakes from my parents. Even from you."

Gina blinked. "What are you saying? You knew about the debts?"

"I knew he was borrowing money to pay bills. But I thought it was a temporary thing. He was always promising me it would get better. He never shared the full extent of it with me. He didn't want to admit he couldn't handle it." She swallowed hard. "I'm so sorry I kept it from you. I did it with the best intentions, but it was wrong. We must be totally honest now with each other, Gina. I know that until now we worked it all out together and we did fine, but we can't have other creditors turn up and risk your new life here, involve your family's property. We need someone who knows all the ins and outs to navigate this for us. How about we go inside and you sit down in the kitchen and we look up a number for debt counseling. Someone professional who can help you sort this out."

Gina bit her lip. "I don't know. Will that cost more money? How can I afford it?"

"We'll look into that. I'm sure we can find a solution." She looked back at the barn. "I'll tell your mother and ask her to play with the girls awhile. We're going to take care of it right away."

"Lily, I feel so miserable." Tears streamed down Gina's cheeks. "My mom, Cade… They will all get into trouble because of me."

"No, they won't." Lily squeezed her

shoulder. "That's exactly why we are getting help. We've tried too long to do everything on our own. We need someone to help us settle this once and for all. We can't have a shadow hanging over your lives all the time. Come on. I'll do the research and make some calls, okay?"

"Thanks, Lily. I don't know what I'd do without you."

CADE DROVE INTO the yard. His shoulders were sore, his neck hurt and his stomach was painfully empty. It sure was the day after. Yesterday he had such a great time and today it was a truckload of work and a reminder of all the responsibilities he had. His mind buzzed with items on the to-do list. The most important one being the conversation with Lily. He hadn't slept much and even while working, his mind had been going over various ways to convince her to stay. But somehow his practical reasons why it would be great didn't ring true. He'd have to tell her how he felt about her. He'd have to take a risk for it. And he had never liked risks.

He rubbed his forehead as he walked up

the steps and into the house. Rosie immediately came to greet him. He brushed her head absentmindedly. From further down the corridor he heard Gina's voice. She was apparently on the phone in the kitchen area. "Yes, I can look that up and send it over to you. Of course as soon as I can." When he came in, Gina looked briefly at him and then took the phone to her own room.

Lily who was at the sink making coffee looked over her shoulder. "Hello. Want coffee?"

"Please." He sank onto a chair. Rosie rested her head on his knee. "What was that all about? Gina looked as if she has been crying."

"She should probably tell you herself, but…there was a man here this morning about debts."

The kinks in Cade's muscles pulled tighter. That was one thing he didn't need right now. "More debts, you mean?" he asked cautiously.

She nodded.

Where was he going to get the money? The bank had just called to say they were thinking about his loan request, because

WINNING OVER THE RANCHER

they were having so many lately and it wasn't feasible to grant them all. His ranch in itself was healthy enough, but after the storm parts of the harvest were lost. Lily's initiatives like the newsletter and Day on the Ranch still had to develop and come to fruition before they could turn a profit. This year would inevitably go down in the books as a meagre one.

How would he get money for Gina? He had promised to help her and he was good on his word, but...

Lily said, "You need not worry about it, Cade." She put a mug of coffee on the table before him and smiled. "I found a very good debt counselor online. Gina is talking to him now. He can work it all out. Make sure she gets payment schedules to meet and that individuals can't threaten her. You don't have to lend money to help her. The ranch won't be affected."

"What?" He tilted his head. "She doesn't need some outsider to meddle in her affairs. We're family, we can help her."

"Yes, she does need an outsider. Someone with an objective view of the situation. Who can advise her without emotions getting mixed into it. We…" Lily swallowed hard. "We should have done that sooner. I helped her after Barry died and… It would just have been better to leave it to a professional."

"No. I want to help her." Cade wanted to get up, but Lily stood in his way. "You're not going to Gina now. She is asking for help and that is a good thing. She can't do this by herself."

"And she doesn't have to, because she has got me."

"You're not Superman. You can't do everything. What do you know about debts?"

"That you can pay them with money."

"Oh, right. When Barry came to me years ago and he said he was in a spot of trouble and could I help him, I fell for it. I loaned him money. My money for my college tuition. He spent it and he never repaid it and when he died I was left with nothing. I had no bachelor's degree, no work experience. Every job I applied for had lots of candidates lined up with better résumés than me. I did everything because I wanted to help him. I did it for family's sake. That was my justification. But it was wrong."

Lily's eyes filled with tears. "I should have told him no. Then he would have looked for help maybe. Now I helped him cover it up and… I don't want you to make the same mistakes. With the best intentions, but nevertheless. You can't help Gina."

"Don't tell me what I can and can't do." The weariness creeping through his bones turned into frustration because she doubted him. He'd lay down his life for his sister and her little ones. "You told me before how I try to make decisions for Gina, but now you're doing the same. She should have told me. I could have helped her."

"I knew you'd say that. Don't you see why I had to do this? Not for Gina, although I want her and the girls to be safe. I did it for you. Because I know how loyal you are. And how stubborn. And how you always feel you must solve everything, by yourself. But it doesn't have to be that way, Cade. You need others. You can rely on others."

No, he couldn't. Because the people he relied on always left. "Really?" he asked in a low voice. "Can I rely on you, Lily? Will you be here next week, next month, next year? Or will you be gone and sitting in Denver or jetting to Dubai, having forgotten all about us?"

"That's not fair, Cade." Her voice almost broke. "I did what I could to ensure Gina and the kids are safe here and now I can continue with my own life. I deserve that chance. I can't stay here because of friendship or the community needing me."

"Of course not. No one is asking you to. I'm just pointing out that…"

The look in her eyes when he said "no one is asking you to" confused him. It almost looked like disappointment. As if she had wanted someone to ask her.

As if she had wanted *him* to ask her?

He tried to refocus on his argument. "My point is that this is our life here and you're leaving again. Shouldn't we decide?"

"I only wanted to protect you. But I see you don't need it." Lily left the kitchen.

ROSIE STARED AFTER her and then looked up at Cade. She whined.

Cade took a deep breath. *No one is asking you?* He hid his face in his hands a moment. He had rehearsed his conversation with Lily a dozen times but this had definitely not been one of the versions. How could it have gone so wrong?

"Cade?" His mother came into the kitchen, a question mark on her features. "I just saw Lily rush to her room in tears. What happened?"

"Nothing special. Just us realizing we are very different." He massaged his temples. "She told me how she felt and…"

"Did you tell her how you feel?"

"Would it make any difference?"

"You won't know unless you try."

"Thanks, Ma, but I think I've tried quite enough for today and all those attempts just made it worse." *So much worse.* He rose quickly. "I can't stay for lunch. I've got work to do."

LILY STOOD IN her bedroom, her eyes closed, her hands clenched into fists by her sides. She took a deep breath to calm down. Didn't they say you had to count until ten? If it helped against anger, it might also help against sadness. Against the overwhelming sense of having lost something she cared for. No one is asking you to stay, he had said.

No. Wasn't that the problem? That she wanted him to ask her to stay? And that if he had, for the right reasons, she might even have considered it? Not for friendship. Not for duty. Only for...

She didn't even want to think the word. She was leaving. She was packing her things and going back to Denver. She'd make up a lie to Gina. Some emergency at work, a colleague needing help with a live presentation or whatever. Gina would believe her. She had no reason to think Cade had anything to do with it. No one had seen the kiss...

The kiss. That wonderful, breathtaking kiss. The moment where she had suddenly started to doubt everything she had believed before. That success could make her happy. That the job in marketing could make her happy. That it could cure loneliness and self-doubt. That it could give connection. Suddenly it had seemed superficial. She needed more. She needed someone to belong with. Not a dream of her own. But a future for the both of them.

But how could she entrust herself to someone who didn't open up?

Lily opened her eyes. She saw everything through the haze of the tears on her lashes. But her mind saw things clearly. Despite their attraction, Cade and she couldn't make it work. He'd never admit he needed her. And she needed to be needed. She needed him, as a reason to stay. Nothing more, nothing less.

Oh, she would still be close to Gina. She would call her and email her and message her and send cards to the girls and presents. She would even set up meetings every now and then. But not here. Not where she might run into Cade. It would be too painful.

My mistake that I fell for him. That I actually started to have feelings for that stubborn silent...

She swallowed hard. She could call him names all she wanted. But her heart told her a different story. It ached; it was broken because of what he had said. That no one was asking her to stay. While that was all she needed to make the choice. She'd give up her dream of the Denver job if she could be with him. She saw that clearly now. But he wouldn't ask. Because he didn't feel the same?

Or because he was afraid?

She didn't know. She could only guess and how could you be in a relationship with someone guessing about their feelings?

No. It had just been a mistake to ever allow herself to feel anything for Cade. It had happened over time and it had taken her by surprise. Because they were polar opposites and she had never thought she could feel so much for someone so different.

But it had been risky. And now she paid the price. The pain eating at her inside. All her hopes of belonging breaking apart.

But it wasn't too late. She could pack her things and go. She could tell herself to shape up. See the truth. She didn't belong here. She was a city girl. Back to Denver it was.

A knock resounded on her door. Mrs. Williams's voice called, "Are you alright, Lily?"

Lily went to the door and opened it a crack. "I'm fine. It was just a big change after yesterday's happy celebratory atmosphere but… I think I gave Gina some good advice and…"

"Oh yes, Gina said the man she talked to was very kind and really listened well and had all kinds of good tips so it seems that this idea of yours will really pay off."

"I'm glad for that." Lily forced a smile. She had to pull it up from her toes, but she cared for these people and she wanted them to be happy. "I'm sorry that I have to leave. I just got a call from work and a colleague of mine has got a really important presentation tomorrow and the colleague who was going to help with it can't make it last minute so they want me to step in. I'll pack my stuff and leave after lunch. Then I should be able to make it and have some prep time. I'm sorry. This is unexpected but…"

"I totally understand. If you want to secure that job, you have to put your best foot forward." Mrs. Williams reached out and squeezed her hand. "You've done so much for us, Lily. You deserve that job. I can't wait for your call that you got it. You are that good."

"Thank you."

Mrs. Williams held her gaze a moment longer. "Cade also wants you to have it. You should know that. He might not say it, he's always been rather uh…tight-lipped about his emotions. But yesterday I heard him talk to people and he was telling everyone what a great job you did. He said he was proud of you."

"Thanks, that's nice to hear." The idea that he was actually proud of her drove new tears to her eyes. She so wanted him to be. *He said it to others. If only he had said it to me.*

"I'd better get packing then," she said softly.

"I'll get you something to eat to take along." Mrs. Williams turned away.

Everything in Lily screamed no at the idea of leaving here. Leaving this house, the friends she had found here and…the sense of belonging she had experienced. But her attraction to Cade made it impossible for her to stay. To even stay as a friend.

It had to be all or nothing and it had turned into nothing. She was going. This very afternoon.

CHAPTER SEVENTEEN

CADE SAT IN the orchard, at the foot of the tree that represented the Williams legacy to him. In the spot where his father had died. He sat there and looked at the grass and thought, as he had thought before, that his father, however young he had been when death snatched him, had died in a good way. Because he had nothing to regret. If he had even in an instant realized that this was it, the end of his life, he had been in the place he loved; he had spent his time with the people he loved; he had made the choices he had wanted to make. His father had of course made mistakes in his lifetime, but in essence he had done it all right. He had known what was important and he had lived by those rules.

As Cade sat there and breathed the scents of the earth and the trees, he wondered what his father would have said of his choices so far. Would he have been proud of the way in which he had kept the ranch going? Would he have said well done, son?

Or would he have thought it should have been done differently?

What would he have made of Gina and the girls coming back home to live here for a while? Of Barry's death and the debts?

What would Dad have made of Lily?

A smile tugged at the corners of his mouth when he imagined how his father would have sat in the kitchen over the newspaper pretending to be reading and then all of a sudden he would have said something. That had been his way. No deep conversations at designated moments, let's sit down and talk. No, a word here and there, during other activities, just in between the ordinary stuff of everyday life. He would have said, "She's a feisty one, Cade, you shouldn't let her get away."

His father wouldn't have seen the differences between Lily and him as a problem. No. He would have thought it an advantage. After all, he had also married a woman who was very different. City versus country, change versus tradition was part of what separated him and Lily, maybe, as their lives up until now had formed their characters. But the real issue went much deeper than that. Was he ready to open up to someone and let them get close to him? Where Lily might see his insecurity and his pain and his fear? Because everything in life was so fragile and it could be swept away from you in an instant, leaving you empty-handed. He had wanted to rush out and fight the storm, but the storm hadn't cared. Death didn't care. It snatched people and left their loved ones in pain. All you could do was steel yourself against it. Build walls. Smile when people asked how you were. Fine. Always fine.

And then Lily had rushed into his life in her red rubber boots. And she had said to him, "You must be heartbroken." And he had been stunned she could actually say that to him, a grown man. But part of him had also known that while he might never put it quite that way, life had dealt him hard knocks and he carried the scars. Lily had expected him to acknowledge that. And he balked at it. He fought it. He hated it. It wasn't Denver standing between them. It was his fear of letting her in. He wanted her to stay on the outside, where he could show her the Cade that he wanted her to see. But it would never work out that way.

He realized something with a breathtaking intensity. No one had asked her to stay. But he should have. He wanted her to be his girl. The woman by his side when things got hard. The one who didn't hesitate to tell him what he did wrong. Who pointed out his mistakes and helped him to do better. He didn't need someone who accepted his walls but who broke them down.

By force if need be.

He exhaled slowly. He had handled it all wrong. And he still didn't know how to do better. Maybe there had been a chance last night when they had kissed. But after all that had been said today… She had a right to tell him she didn't want to consider a relationship anymore.

Wasn't it too late?

"Uncle Cade!" Stacey came running toward him. He opened his arms and she ran straight into them and hit her face against his shoulder. "Auntie Lily is leaving. She says she has to. But I don't want her to. Not today, not ever. Can't you make her stay?"

His gut clenched. "When did she say that?"

"Grandma is making food for her to take. And she's packing. I don't want her to go. Please help me make her stay." Stacey rubbed her face against him, putting on her most pleading "I truly want this" voice.

But he didn't need convincing. He needed Lily. Yes, he knew now that if she left things would be different here. His work less fulfilling, his prospects empty. He had fought so hard to keep her at arm's length so he need not admit how much she had come to mean to him. Because he had been afraid to lose her. To lose her to the city or her career. But fact was that he was losing her because of his own reluctance to say what he really should have said to her. It was short and sweet. It didn't need much rehearsing either.

Just a lot of courage.

A leap of faith.

"Can you help me with a little surprise?" he asked Stacey. "A way to ask Lily to stay with us."

"Really? Sure." Stacey nodded earnestly.

Cade said, "I need to get a few things for it. Now you go and tell Lily that she can't leave without having seen the orchard. Tell her it's really important. Make sure she comes here in say…fifteen minutes?"

Stacey nodded. "I'll go tell her now. And if she wants to leave anyway, I'll ask Grandma to stop her. She always knows how to do things."

I'm glad someone here knows, Cade thought as he scrambled to his feet and brushed the grass off his knees. His heart beat in his throat. Fifteen minutes to get this right. But it wasn't up to him now. It was up to Lily. And what she'd decide.

CHAPTER EIGHTEEN

"But I don't see why I should," Lily said. "I'm all packed and ready to go. I really need to be on the road and…" She couldn't stand here much longer without crying. Gina had been super surprised that she wanted to leave and had even asked if it was her fault. Mrs. Williams had packed her fresh banana bread as a sweet treat to take home and… They were all so sweet.

Stacey said, "You really should. It's mega important. I'll take you there." She slipped her small hand in Lily's palm. "Come on." She walked her to the orchard's entrance. "You have to go and see the big tree. The family tree."

No, she didn't want to see anything that had to do with family. She didn't want to be reminded of the way she had been received here, the warm welcome, the good feeling she had had about it from day one. She didn't want memories to fill her head and eat away at her resolve to leave. She didn't want that small voice asking her if this was the best thing to do grow any louder.

Most of all, she didn't want to run into Cade.

Stacey led her into the orchard and then pointed. "Go on. I can't come with you. I'll see you later." Her eyes danced with a secret amusement.

What is she up to? "I don't know if…" Lily fumbled.

"Go on. It's a surprise." Stacey giggled and skipped away.

Lily listened to the rustle of the breeze in the leaves and the distant birdsong. This was a beautiful place. A place that spoke to her heart. Why not say goodbye to it? Even if it was with tears in her eyes?

She walked down the path forcing herself to hold her arms by her side and breathe deeply. To savor the moment no matter how much her brain shouted to run away. She had come here to work, but she had learned how to live. To go slow for a change and live in the moment. It was a beautiful experience that would always stay with her.

She saw the big tree in the distance. She blinked. Was she seeing that right? There were flowers in the grass, laid out to form colorful letters. They said…

Stay with me.

She frowned. How had the flowers ended up in the orchard? There was no one…

Cade stepped from behind the tree. He stood there like he had the first time she had seen him on the land. A strong resilient figure. A lone cowboy on guard. Someone to depend on. Someone who was also used to fending for himself. Someone who might be hard to read and get close to.

He stood there looking at her. He didn't say anything, he didn't even smile. And she saw the pain in his eyes and the tightness of his jaws. He was actually afraid of how she might respond. That she would turn around and walk away and leave him.

Cade said, "Lily, when you first came here, you completely took me by surprise. I had some prejudices about you, about city people in general, and how you knew nothing about country ways, but you proved me wrong on all accounts. You won hearts wherever you went and…it was so easy for me to like you, to fall for you. But I didn't want that to happen. I knew from the start you were leaving. That was the whole point, right? The festival here was your ticket to success in the city and… Why fall in love? You'd never stay. You'd have to give up so much for it and…what for? This guy who is always working? Who is so used to being the troubleshooter, the problem fixer that he forgot how to ask for anything for himself. That he even forgot who he is, outside of work."

"That's not true." Lily stepped closer. "You're far more than just the successful rancher or the regional representative or the loving son and brother. You can be silly and you love music and you're a good dancer. And you should more often just take a minute to grab some apple honey ice cream. Without answering your phone."

Cade nodded slowly. "It's not much fun to make music alone. And for dancing you definitely need two people. Now, Lily…" He looked her in the eye. "I feel so bad asking this of you. Because I know what you sacrificed already. You left college without a bachelor's degree to help out at the pizzeria, for a little while, they said. But it turned into years. You did it out of love, I know that. You always put yourself in second place. I don't want you to do that again. I want you to have that big career and all the things you dreamed of."

That he saw how important it was to her, meant the world. He could have tried to make it less attractive to get her to stay, but he didn't. Cade was honest to a fault. That was one of the reasons why she cared so much for him.

Cade continued, "If you…get into a relationship with me, you're going to be with someone who has a ton of responsibilities. This ranch takes a lot of time. There are seasons so busy that I'm up from dawn to dusk. Even at night a call can come in from a friend in need. We all help each other here. That is the country way. I love it. I like to be busy. And I love this ranch. It's my family legacy. It's where I think of my father most every day. If you stay, we need to figure out how I can make time for you. Because that's what I want to do. Make you my top priority. My number one."

Lily felt tears in her eyes. Him saying

that, especially in this place, was everything she wanted to hear. "I won't lie and say giving up my Denver dreams is easy. Organizing Apple Fest emphasized what I love about that job and that I'm good at it. But I realized what really motivated me to try so hard. To prove myself. To be worthy. And a career, no matter how fulfilling, could never have given me that validation. Only connection can. Being with people you love. You have that here on the family ranch. You are in the place where you belong. And I want to belong like that. What I experienced here during my stay is what I've been looking for, without even knowing it myself."

"Still it will be a hard life sometimes," Cade said. "A struggle to get through bad seasons. Or just to fit in time away from work. I can't whisk you away on a surprise weekend because I can't just leave the ranch. Things like that have to be arranged for well in advance, and maybe it would sort of kill the romance for you."

Lily smiled. "It needn't be that complicated. Just time for us, grabbed where we can find it. Doesn't have to be an entire weekend. How about…just half an hour at night where we walk in this orchard hand in hand and chat? Or sit on the porch or… look at the stars?"

Cade tilted his head. "You mean that? Are you seriously considering…"

Lily said, "Turn away for a sec. I'll tell you when you can look again."

"What? Why?"

"Don't ask questions just do what I ask you."

CADE TURNED HIS back on her. His heart hammered hard. His head was full of racing thoughts and all he could think was that he should have said different things. Or just wrapped his arms around her and kissed her silly. Maybe the attraction between them could convince her it was worth a try?

When you ask her to give up her dreams for you? his rational mind asked. *Wake up, Cade.*

But didn't they agree on the most important thing in life? Their love of family and their need for a safe haven, a base to build on?

"You can look," Lily said.

He waited a few heartbeats before turning around. He didn't know what she planned or wanted, but it made his knees tremble. He looked at her first, then at the ground in front of her. She had rearranged his flowers. It no longer said stay with me, but they formed a heart with one word in it. *Yes*.

Not *yes maybe*, not *yes but*, not *yes on condition that*. Well, maybe she didn't have enough flowers for that last one...

He had to laugh involuntarily.

"Are you laughing at me?" Lily asked. Her eyes were a little moist, but they also twinkled.

"No, at my own thoughts. How I sort of expected you to need a report as long as my arm to set up the conditions of us ever being together and you simply say yes?"

"Because it means too much to walk away from it." Lily held his gaze. "When I came here, I was on a quest to find what I could do now that I was cut loose from all the obligations that had dominated my life for so long. And it seemed so logical that it was what I had wanted before. Working in marketing, an apartment, a set of friends, nice hobbies. I had figured it all out for myself. Then I came here and...doubts began to niggle in the back of my mind. I've always lived in the city, but I've never liked bustling crowds. I feel happy when I am in nature. That's why I started rock climbing. I practice indoors, but I want to get good enough to do it outdoors in a place where I can find peace and quiet. And you know, I may feel like the pizzeria always took too much time away from us as a family, but it also created a bond. We had something to work for together. We were proud of what we achieved together. After the pizzeria was sold off I missed that. I was looking for a way to regain that sense of...meaning. I found it here. On this ranch where you have a family tradition going back generations."

Her eyes filled with tears. "I felt so cut loose when I came here, Cade. I never wanted to admit it to myself, but I was drifting. I wanted to get back in touch with Gina because...we were friends and sisters and we had the communal garden and the rescue pets and... I missed all that so much. Here I found it again and...there was you. I couldn't really understand you and at times I was about to throttle you, but... I also felt safe with you. In the place where I belong. And I don't want to lose that feeling again."

He reached out and brushed his hand down her cheek. "You must remember one thing, Lily. I may not always know just what to say, but I do need you. After you said you were leaving, it felt so empty here. I knew I had been a big knucklehead."

Now Lily laughed out loud. "Yes, you were. But let's forget about that now. I'll gather up these flowers and put them in a vase before they wilt."

He watched as she collected them into her arm. "It all started with that, you know. How you picked up those broken flowers after the storm, as if they were so precious to you. I saw someone love my livelihood as much as I love it. I guess then it happened, even if I didn't know it yet. And wouldn't have acknowledged it for the world."

She stood in front of him with her arms full of flowers, beaming at him.

"So you're not leaving after all?" he asked, just to make sure.

"I'm not going anywhere."

"That's what I wanted to hear." He leaned in and kissed her.

EPILOGUE

"THERE." LILY STEPPED back and held a hand over the little screen on her camera to keep the sun off so she could see the images she had just shot. The orchards were in full bloom and with the blue skies above and the bright sunshine, she could get amazing images for the next newsletter. All the beautiful blossoming trees shouted spring, and energy for the new season buzzed through her system. She had so many ideas to grow the newsletter readership and the ranch's reach on social media. Cade sometimes said he didn't know how she came up with it. "What's your secret?" he'd tease her. And she'd know, deep down inside, that he was the secret. Her love for him, her happiness that they were together. It warmed her, it was a never ending source of inspiration.

She lowered the camera with a happy

sigh. She just wanted to take a quick look at the old family tree, the heart of the orchard, and then she'd head back to the house for coffee. With a little luck Mrs. Williams, or Ma, as she called her these days, would have something sweet in the oven: her famous chocolate chip cookies or cake, or the banana bread she had been treated to the very first day she came here. The day her life had changed, even if she hadn't known it yet.

Lily enjoyed the feel of the soft grass under her feet as she walked to the old tree. It looked even more majestic after the damage done in the storm that had brought her here. Authentic and strong because it had remained standing despite it all. It was the symbol of the Williams ancestors who had first settled here, started the ranch, built their livelihood. It blossomed too, maybe not as lush as the younger trees who were almost exuberant in their spring display, but it produced flowers in measure, to show it was still alive, and could still bear fruit. It fulfilled its purpose.

She closed the distance and put her hand against the rough bark. She smiled as she spoke to the tree without words, letting it know she was happy to be here. That she was happy because love was here.

Then her gaze fell to something caught in the fork of the branches. It was dark blue. She reached for it on impulse, her fingertips brushing something soft. Velvet. It was a small…box? She caught hold of it and pulled it free, held it in her palm. Was it some surprise from Cade? Had he left it here for her to find?

But it wasn't her birthday…

She opened it, fully expecting to see a pendant for a necklace or some other shiny thing. But nothing could have prepared her for the glitter of gold in the sunshine and the sparkle of the small diamond in the ring.

A ring!

"Lily."

She turned to Cade's warm voice. She drank in his appearance from his neatly brushed-back hair to his crisp shirt and mud-free boots. He smiled at her, with that slow smile she found so enticing. Then he lowered one knee to the grass.

This was it. This was… Goose bumps

skittered across her arms and tears pushed behind her eyes.

His smile intensified. "I had thought up this entire speech to say. I practiced it all night. But I can't remember a single word of it. I know just this. You came and you changed my life. You mean everything to me. Do you want to marry me?"

"Yes." Clutching the open ring box, Lily threw herself into Cade's arms. He almost lost his balance, still half kneeling in the grass. They laughed. The sound echoed through the orchard. This was how it was supposed to be: a place of laughter, warmth, belonging. A place to feel safe and accepted. A place where love grew.

No matter how many storms had battered it, trying to destroy it, the orchard had survived. It was in bloom and they were at the heart of it, holding on to each other, knowing that as long as they kept doing that, they'd conquer anything.

Together.

* * * * *

ACKNOWLEDGMENTS

As ALWAYS, thanks to all authors (especially Harlequin authors), editors and agents who share online about the writing and publishing process. Special mention goes to the Write for Harlequin website which is a goldmine of information. There I read that Heartwarming was especially looking for Western stories and the first seed was planted for my Heroes of the Rockies series. My amazing agent, Jill Marsal, helped me shape the proposal and it landed in the capable hands of my wonderful editors, Adrienne Macintosh and Natalia Castano, whose feedback is always spot on. Thanks also to the rest of the dedicated team at Heartwarming, especially Kathleen Scheibling for her input on the proposal, and the cover design team for the evocative cover.

The small town of Heartmont is fictional but inspired by real-life towns in Colorado's apple country and there are actual apple festivals organized in fall. As a huge fan of festivals with arts, crafts and music, I loved creating my own as the perfect backdrop for the hero and heroine's budding romance. Now I'm already back in Heartmont to give another couple their happily-ever-after and hope you will also want to return. Happy reading!

Get 3 FREE REWARDS!

We'll send you 2 FREE Books plus a FREE Mystery Gift.

FREE
Value Over
$20

Both the **Love Inspired**® and **Love Inspired**® Suspense series feature compelling novels filled with inspirational romance, faith, forgiveness and hope.

THE NORA ROBERTS COLLECTION

Get to the heart of happily-ever-after in these Nora Roberts classics! Immerse yourself in the beauty of love by picking up this incredible collection written by, legendary author, Nora Roberts!

COMING NEXT MONTH FROM

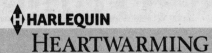

HARLEQUIN
HEARTWARMING

#487 THEIR SURPRISE ISLAND WEDDING
Hawaiian Reunions • by Anna J. Stewart
Workaholic Marella Benoit doesn't know how to have fun,
even at her sister's Hawaiian wedding! Thankfully surfer
Keane Harper can help. He'll show Marella how to embrace the
magic of the islands—but will she embrace his feelings for her?

#488 A SWEET MONTANA CHRISTMAS
The Cowgirls of Larkspur Valley • by Jeannie Watt
Getting jilted before her wedding is bad enough, but now
Maddie Kincaid is unexpectedly spending the holidays on a
guest ranch with bronc rider Sean Arteaga. 'Tis the season to
start over—maybe even with Sean by her side...

#489 HER COWBOY'S PROMISE
The Fortunes of Prospect • by Cheryl Harper
The history at the Majestic Prospect Lodge isn't limited to just
the building—Jordan and Clay have a past, and now they're
working together to restore the lodge's former glory. But it'll
take more than that to mend their hearts...

#490 THE COWBOY AND THE COACH
Love, Oregon • by Anna Grace
Violet Fareas is more than ready for her new job coaching
high school football. But convincing the community that she's
capable—and trying to resist Ash Wallace, the father of her star
player—is a whole new ball game!

HWCNM0823

HARLEQUIN
PLUS

Try the best multimedia subscription service for romance readers like you!

Read, Watch and Play.

Experience the easiest way to get the romance content you crave.

Start your **FREE TRIAL** at
<u>www.harlequinplus.com/freetrial</u>.